PENGUIN BOOKS
Hand on the Sun

Tariq Mehmood came to Britain in the early sixties and attended junior and comprehensive schools in Bradford. After leaving home at an early age he became involved with various radical political groups. As a result of the disturbances in Bradford during the summer of 1981, the author was put on trial as one of the Bradford Twelve. He conducted his own defence and was subsequently acquitted. *Hand on the Sun* is his first book and shows him to be a writer of considerable promise.

D1380411

Tariq Mehmood

Hand on the Sun

PENGUIN BOOKS

Penguin Books Ltd, Harmondsworth, Middlesex, England
Penguin Books, 40 West 23rd Street, New York, New York, 10010, U.S.A.
Penguin Books Australia Ltd, Ringwood, Victoria, Australia
Penguin Books Canada Ltd, 2801 John Street, Markham, Ontario, Canada
L3R 1B4
Penguin Books (N.Z.) Ltd, 182–190 Wairau Road, Auckland 10, New Zealand

First published 1983

Copyright © Tariq Mehmood, 1983
All rights reserved

Made and printed in Great Britain by
Richard Clay (The Chaucer Press) Ltd, Bungay, Suffolk
Set in Times

Except in the United States of America, this book is sold subject
to the condition that it shall not, by way of trade or otherwise, be lent,
re-sold, hired out, or otherwise circulated without the
publisher's prior consent in any form of binding or cover other than
that in which it is published and without a similar condition
including this condition being imposed on the subsequent purchaser

To Phyl and Ejaz
For all oppressed and struggling people

'To hold a people down forever is like putting a hand on the sun.'

El Salvadorian graffiti

Glossary

ammi-ji   dear mother
Aslam-O-Alaikum   Muslim greeting: 'Peace be upon you'
Azaan   mullah's call to prayer
baba ji   term of respect
billi   cat
biradari   extended family
budda   old man
chakkar   a trick, fiddle; also a circle
chamchas   henchmen, lackeys
choudhary   well-to-do person
dahl   curried pulses
dallay   pimp, ponce
danda   baton
danga   horse-drawn carriage
dholki   drum
doli   bridal carriage
dulhan   bride
dupatta   veil, scarf
gherao   encirclement; a form of picketing
ghoonday   thugs
gitaran   guitars
gora   white man
goree   white woman
guli danda   Indo-Pak game
gurdwara   Sikh temple
haram zada   illegitimate, bastard
harami   bastard
Heer   famous Punjabi lovers
hoor   mythical woman of paradise
izzat   honour
jutian   spankers, slippers
kala   black

kameez   shirt
khassum   husband
kothi   big bungalow
Khuda hafiz   God be with you
kurta   shirt
ladoo   sweet
maila   fair
maim   white woman
marabaa, measurement of land: 24 acres
mather choud   motherfucker
mirchan   chillies
ohai sohaniay   how are you, beautiful?
parandha   black band in woman's hair
paratha   type of bread
pardesi   someone who is in a far-off land
parna   scarf
Ranjha   famous Punjabi lover
roti   bread
sajno   friends
salwar   north Indian woman's trousers
sarkari   official
slam   Muslim greeting
Siparas   chapters of the Koran
tawa   roasting pan
tokras   baskets
Wahay Guru   Sikh religious salutation
Wallait   England
wothti   wife
yaar   friend
zinda baad   long live

Chapter 1

The music of a well coordinated hymn had just faded away. The assembly hall of a comprehensive school, with many children standing in military fashion, was what it faded into. The Headmaster looked down on the segregated rows of girls, boys and blacks. His eyes travelled from the girls, to the boys, to the blacks. The blacks at the back of the hall held his gaze. He toyed with them in his thoughts for a moment. 'They come to our country but they cling to their backward ideals,' he thought, as his eyes passed from meaningless face to meaningless face. He felt pity for them, living in a strange land, not being able to speak the land's language. Their parents were poor but it was better than what they would get in their own country. He satisfied himself with the thought that he at least was helping these mishaps of civilization, these abortions of Great Britain. His eyes travelled into the ranks of the boys.

The religious education teacher read out his sermon. There were some, he thought, as he looked on the few blacks who stood in with the boys, who saw sense. They must learn to integrate. They must accept that they are in our country. The sermon came to an end. The Headmaster gave his much-delivered speech. The boredom of the pupils was beginning to turn to frustration.

In the back, Jalib fired a pellet into the girls. Then he turned his smiling face into a mask of perfect innocence. A girl yelled.

'Who did that?' thundered the Headmaster. A deathly silence followed. He walked down from his platform to a row of petrified Asians. 'Which one of you did that?' No answer. The children, all of them, were looking to the back of the hall. 'Stand straight, the rest of you,' he roared. At once his command was obeyed. 'I said, which one of you did that? Who was it, Carol?' he asked the victim.

'Don't know, sir.'

Turning back to the Asians, he said, 'When the assembly is

over, I want all of you to stay behind.' He returned to the platform.

Slowly the rest of the children marched to their classrooms. Their glances showed they felt the Asians deserved what was coming. Jim passed them. Jim was the 'cock of the school'. 'You're going to get it, woggies! Go back home!' he laughed, joined by his friends. 'Wait till we get hold of you, you black cunts!' He walked on. Jalib stuck up two fingers at him. 'I'll see you at break time, you fucking Paki,' said Jim.

The hall was deserted now, except for the Asians. The Headmaster came to them. 'Stay here until I return.' He left in an air of mystery. Like the cloak of Dracula, his black cloak followed him. But there was no mystery. They all knew he had gone for the cane. They knew also that no one would split on Jalib. Jalib felt pride in that thought. An eternity passed.

A lump of guilt was forming in Jalib's thoughts. Should he admit his offence and save everyone else a caning? He didn't have time to decide. The Headmaster, cane in hand, marched up to the frightened children, like an army general approaching a regiment of deserters. He approached the first boy, who held out his hand. Crack! Mohan cried out.

'It was me, sir! It was me!' shouted Jalib, unable to control his guilt, unable to see his friend suffer.

'I thought so. I bloody thought so,' smiled the Headmaster. He walked towards Jalib. Jalib gritted his teeth.

'Two for you, my boy,' he said. He turned to the rest of the pupils. 'Let this be a lesson to all of you. You are no longer in a jungle. This is a civilized country. I don't know what you do in your countries but here we do not throw things at ladies.'

'Shit,' whispered Mohan.

All the children were aware of Jalib's offence, but even so none doubted his innocence. Crack! He became their hero for the day.

The Headmaster brandished the cane at the children and said, 'If any one of you does this sort of thing again, I will cane each of you and inform your parents that you are molesting these young ladies!' Crack! An unusual silence spread over the group. All were aware what the consequences of that threat would be. Their parents would never tolerate such behaviour. It was immoral. Caning at school meant beating at home and humiliation in front of their friends. 'Now get to your bloody classes!' roared the Headmaster. The children moved off quickly.

Mohan walked up to Jalib and put his arm around Jalib's shoulders. 'What you do that for?' he asked. A lone tear rolled down Jalib's cheek. It was followed by a flood. 'Don't tell anyone about this,' he asked, referring to his tears. 'Shit. I fucking won't!' promised Mohan.

They walked up the steps and along a corridor to their classroom. Hand in hand, like long-separated lovers, they walked closely side by side.

Jim came out of the toilet. He was tall – five foot eight – with ginger hair that had always amused the Asian children. He had a foolish air of arrogance. He was fat and everyone in the school was scared of him. He had fought many fights and never lost one. His was a hard-earned position. He confronted Jalib and Mohan, his arms crossed, like a wrestler.

'Now listen, you queers, I want to see you at break or else there'll be worse, you fucking Pakis!' He laughed and smashed his way past Jalib and Mohan.

'Fucking *gora*,' both of them said. They burst out laughing. Their laughter changed from laughing at Jim – they were used to his bullying – to hysterical laughter. They were going to an English lesson, yet both spoke English as well as any white pupil their age. The teacher would try to teach them English, they would talk deliberately in Punjabi. Usually they pretended to talk to each other. In fact, they swore at the teacher, at the Headmaster, at the whole school system. When they reached the classroom, they were still laughing hysterically.

Mohan knocked on the door and walked in, all traces of laughter gone. In its place, a look of stupid ignorance.

'So you've been naughty again, Jalib,' joked Mr Ramsey. (The Asian pupils called him Mr Rami, the Punjabi word for 'bastard'.)

Jalib and Mohan quietly walked to their desks and Ramsey continued teaching. The pupils, for their part, continued to refuse to listen.

Jalib's thoughts were of the break. Jim was big. Jalib could not defeat him in a one-to-one fight. He could never let Mohan or any of his other friends join in if it was a man-to-man duel. Jalib saw himself lying in a pool of his own blood, his nose broken, the whites laughing, his own friends embarrassed as he lost to a *gora*. His parents would beat him, of course. The Headmaster would never believe he didn't start the fight. Jalib felt the world turn against him. He too would be added to the list of Jim's vanquished. He thought, 'I could faint in class. That would make Rami send me to the matron.' But he knew he had to fight, whether he won or lost, for such was the law of this jungle. If he didn't fight, no one would talk to him. He would be an outcast. A coward. With pleading eyes, he looked to Mohan.

Mohan was doodling on his notebook, trying to ease the tension building up inside him. 'If that fucking *gora* gets Jalib down, I'll kick him in his balls!' he thought, knowing that would never happen. The law was that fights were one-to-one. Besides, the implications of Mohan joining in were too dangerous. It could have repercussions on others who had nothing to do with the dispute. Mohan's body burnt in anger, his impotence nearly reducing him to tears. His hands were beginning to shake. Quickly, he checked his emotions. He looked across at Jalib. 'How can that bloody skeleton win . . . He should eat more chapattis,' he thought, trying to force a smile.

Well aware that no one was listening to a word he said, Ramsey carried on unperturbed. Jalib searched Mohan's eyes for a moment. Sensing Mohan's feeling, his thoughts about fainting and trying to avoid the fight embarrassed him. He blinked and quickly looked out the window.

The playground was deserted. The trees in the background made the school look like a lost paradise. Cows grazed in the field beyond it. They took Jalib's thoughts back to his village, away from the trouble he faced. How *goras* were loved there! He wondered what the time was there. 'Maybe they are asleep now,' he smiled, remembering how he had expected to see gold everywhere in this country. Suddenly his dream ended. The morning bell rang, signalling the break. Instantly there was a commotion of closing books, moving chairs, opening desk lids. Outside, the noise of children talking, shouting, running to the playground.

'Do Exercise 12 for the next lesson,' said Ramsey with an indifferent voice. He left the room without noticing that today none of the pupils left before him. All eyes turned to Jalib who looked like a terrified mouse in front of hungry cats. Trapped.

'I'm going to fight that motherfucker!' shouted Jalib in Punjabi.

'*Zinda baad*, Jalib!' roared his friends, some smiling, others excited, as if they were about to see the World Heavyweight Boxing Championship. They left the room.

Mohan stopped to shake Jalib's hand, as a gesture of good luck. Jalib quickly withdrew his hand, wiped the sweat from it and shook hands with all twenty of his class fellows.

About a hundred children had gathered in the playground. Jim stood in the middle of them, his arms folded across his chest, smiling. 'This Paki's nowt,' he thought. A massive circle was made by the crowd of spectators. The gladiators prepared for their battle.

Mohan had managed to get behind Jim. 'He's got a knife! He's going to cut your balls off!' whispered Mohan in Jim's ear.

'Get the black bastard, Jim!' shouted another voice. The whole crowd roared with laughter. Jalib clenched his fists, the fear turning to anger.

'Don't worry, you can't get a black eye – you've already got two!' The crowd laughed. 'Go on, Jim! What are you waiting for?' a voice yelled.

Jim stood paralysed. He felt his testicles, fear gripping him. 'Come on, then,' challenged Jalib, realizing he had some unknown advantage over Jim. His body filled with strength.

Jim's fear turned to frustration. He moved forward. The crowd cheered him. He stopped. Jalib's heart suddenly jumped. He got ready, then relaxed.

'The bastard's got a knife!' cried Jim. His frustration brought tears to his eyes.

'Break it up, you lot! Who's fighting?' shouted some teachers, smashing their way through the crowd. Within seconds, the crowd evaporated.

'Who was fighting?' the teacher asked a first former.

'Him, sir,' pointing to Jalib.

'Right, son, come here,' he said, dragging Jalib by the collar. 'Who were you fighting?' he asked.

Jalib was full of pride and joy. He would be considered the 'cock of the school' now. 'No one, sir,' he lied, frightened again at the thought of what he was to receive.

'I've no time to argue. Go to Mr English's office immediately.'

Jalib looked around to see if he could find a sympathetic face. Mohan had retreated to the far corner of the playground and was pretending to talk to friends.

'Okay – you,' a teacher said to a first former, 'come here!'

'Yes, sir?' replied the first former politely.

'Who was fighting with this one?' asked the teacher.

'Big Jim, sir.'

Big Jim was nowhere to be seen. 'You go to the Headmaster's office now, I'll find Jim.' Jalib bowed his head and walked towards the school. At least he had shown courage. He had stood up to the 'cock of the school'. 'Why didn't he get me?' he wondered. He had not heard Jim screaming about the knife.

Jalib rang the Headmaster's bell. There was no answer. At the sound of familiar footsteps, he turned round with fear. It was Jim. Jalib looked at Jim, with smiling eyes. 'Dracula' appeared from round the corner. Suddenly the two gladiators didn't hate each other any more – they had a common enemy and there was a solidarity between them.

'Come in.' The Headmaster sat down behind his desk. Behind him was a large green plant. It had the look of a Triffid, ready to strike. 'Who started it?' asked the Headmaster. No reply. 'You, boy,' looking at Jalib. 'You really are a trouble-maker. Have you forgotten the caning you got? You want another dose, do you?

'You, Jim, you really ought to know better. You're a big lad now. You'll be leaving school next year. Now, what was the point of the fight? Do you think you have done something good?' Jim had lowered his eyes. There was no reply. 'Who started it?' Silence. 'Who started the fight?' roared the Headmaster at Jim. 'He did, sir,' said Jim, wiping tears from his eyes.

'No I didn't, sir! Honest! He did!' replied Jalib who, on seeing Jim cry, determined not to. 'Very well, bend over both of you!' The Headmaster opened his desk and pulled out a well-worn implement, an old plimsoll, much practised in the art of striking bums. With the world upside down, the fighters looked at each other, smiled. Crack! Crack! Jalib felt a fire start in his backside, travel down through his head and out on to the floor. He yelled. Crack! Crack! Jim's face reddened. 'Stand up straight!' ordered the Headmaster. 'Now shake hands.' They obeyed. 'Apologize to each other.' Command obeyed. The handshake was meaningless. With the punishment over, the solidarity broke. There would be trouble.

Jim was aware by now that he had been tricked. There had been no knife. He wanted vengeance. He had been humiliated in

14

front of the whole school. 'These wogs always stick together,' he thought.

'Now go to your classes,' ordered the Headmaster as he seated himself in his chair.

'We pals again, Big Jim?' asked Jalib. The red-faced bully closed the door behind them. 'Yeah,' replied the lying voice. They walked off in opposite directions.

'You really showed that fucking *gora*, Jalib,' congratulated Ranjit. He had been Big Jim's last victim. His face still bore the marks of defeat. Every time he looked in the mirror, Ranjit remembered the fight. Big Jim on top of him, Ranjit struggling under his weight. 'Say sorry. Say sorry, you fucking wog or I'll break your nose!' Ranjit had been talking to a white girl earlier that day. The white boys, particularly the big ones, hated him for talking to her. Big Jim kept punching him. Eventually he scratched Ranjit's face, kicked him and walked away laughing. Ranjit's scar would be a permanent reminder of his defeat and humiliation. Like all their friends, he was proud of Jalib.

Mohan, Jalib and Ranjit were standing in the covered area of the playground. It was like a big veranda. When it rained heavily, the P E teacher held exercises there. Its walls were covered with graffiti – 'Wogs go home', 'Black bastards'. These words were common in the language of most of the white kids and a constant reminder to the black kids of the feelings of the school. The three stood in the corner, laughing at what Mohan had done to scare Big Jim. It was a great day for them. In their excitement they forgot about having their lunch.

'Do you think he'll try owt again?' asked Mohan.

'Don't care!' replied Jalib.

'He's not going to give up,' said Ranjit. He had fought and lost to Jim and felt he had a better understanding of him. Ranjit felt sorry for Jalib, knowing he was no match for Jim. They all understood. A silence crept over them; their impotence burned. Education and schooling seemed so far away from this reality. The peaceful scenes around the school mocked their existence.

Cold fear ran through Jalib's body. Big Jim was walking towards them. He had six other boys with him and was followed by an army of spectators, all white. 'You dirty black bastards, I'm going to teach you all a lesson!' he roared. 'You –' pointing to Mohan, 'you've got something special, boy.' All three were paralysed. 'So many all together,' thought Jalib. He felt a pain rip through his mouth; as his head turned he saw Mohan on the floor. Ranjit was rolling in agony as feet went into his stomach. Jalib tried to hit Jim. Someone pulled his hair. Jim kicked him in his testicles. There was blood running down his face. Through the blood he saw Ranjit, mouth open, his front teeth missing. The crowd was laughing. Jalib dived at someone. He was delirious. He could see many faces blurred. He was being thrown from one side to another. 'Ranjit!' They were hitting him now. Jalib could not feel his body. 'Mohan!' Each time he called out a name, the crowd roared. He could not make out what they were saying. His eyes were beginning to close. Suddenly the crowd vanished.

Mohan was clutching his testicles, yelling. Jalib and Ranjit were covered in blood. They picked Mohan up. He screamed louder. 'Stay with him. I'll get the matron,' said Ranjit, spitting blood. He walked into the school.

The matron and two teachers arrived. Ranjit wasn't with them. 'You've been fighting again, Jalib!' said a teacher. 'Every day you cause trouble. Do your parents know what you get up to at school? You're not in a jungle now, boy. Be thankful you're here. You'd be keeping donkeys up in the mountains back home. This won't be the end of the matter! You think I feel sorry for you because you are bleeding . . .?'

'No, sir. Please help him.'

Mohan was sobbing now. The teachers picked him up. The matron gave Jalib a quick inspection. 'Just a small cut. Move, boy! Don't stand there like a monkey!' Jalib ran in front of them. As he approached the school entrance, every window had a face, all staring down. Jalib bowed his head.

Matron wiped the blood from them. Mohan had recovered. They knew there would be trouble at home. There was silence as they cleaned the stains from their clothes, all with one thought . . . vengeance.

The matron returned, 'I have had a word with the Headmaster. You must go home now. We don't want any more trouble. We will contact your parents. You must report to the Headmaster immediately after assembly tomorrow.' She handed them their satchels. They got up and walked quietly out of the school.

'We gonna wait for the rest?' asked Mohan, referring to the other Asian kids. 'We'll see 'em in town,' answered Jalib.

They waited in silence at the bus stop where everyone got off. The bus arrived, very late. Children descended, a few white, the rest black. 'We got the bastards!' said a voice. 'We taught those white bastards a lesson!' There was a large group of black kids, all talking and shouting.

Big Jim had bragged about how he beat the three of them up single-handed. But word got round that a crowd of white boys had ganged up on Jalib, Mohan and Ranjit. After school, in the bus queue, a fight had developed. No one quite knew how. Big Jim and a few other white kids had been shouting abuse, as usual. It was expected. Those who did not take part were shunned by the others. This time Big Jim and his friends had been chased away from the bus queue. They had promised retaliation.

'There's going to be trouble tomorrow,' said Ranjit. 'Let's give it to them!' Everyone shouted agreement. All knew that a big fight had to come. It was the only answer.

'Get some pepper and weapons,' ordered Jalib. 'We'll show these bastards they can't beat us and get away with it.' It was no longer a personal fight with Big Jim. He was merely a catalyst for what had been brewing for a long time. After plans were made, the group drifted homewards.

Chapter 2

Jalib and Ranjit were left alone after the crowd disappeared. People passed; some were smiling. An old woman fed bread to pigeons. Jalib's eyes travelled from face to face. 'How could all these people not know what happened to us?' he wondered.

'What you going to tell your father, Ranjit?' Jalib asked.

'He'll have gone to work by the time I get home. With luck I won't see him until Saturday. Then I suppose I'll try to make him understand — and get a beating.' Ranjit's father worked in a textile mill, twelve hours a night. Ranjit really had no idea what a mill was. He only saw his father at weekends and then they usually had guests. His father, when he had the time, preferred to talk to him about what life was like in India. Once he told Ranjit about the days of the Raj. Ranjit had heard the word often but did not understand what it meant. He knew that the *goras* were in India for a long time, but not why. He had often wondered if the *goras* were treated, in India, the same way he and his family were treated here.

'Say hello to your father as you get some *jutian*,' joked Ranjit, walking away. It was getting late.

'Yeah, see you tomorrow.' Jalib headed towards his bus stop, then decided to walk home. The thought of what would happen at home frightened him. His father would shout and beat him. His mother would cry. He would never be able to explain what had happened.

He had been so happy in Pakistan. He saw himself again in the village; the sun was out, he was sitting in the shade of a large tree. He always used to sit there. It was a very old tree. The noise of parrots singing their songs at the top of the tree always amused him. He heard the mullah giving his *Azaan*. He saw his friends playing *guli danda*. They used to swim in a small stream, even though they were told it was dangerous.

The stream was about half a mile from the village. During the monsoons the whole area flooded. Beyond the stream, in the distance, were tall hills, broken here and there by erosion. A railway line ran between the hills. There was a graveyard on the plateau of one of the hills and villagers would talk for hours about who was buried there. It was said that many white men were buried there. This information had always puzzled Jalib: what were white men doing out in the countryside, so far from any major town?

Jalib had spent many hours in the shade of the tree overhanging the cliff by the stream. Older boys would copy the *goras*. They would buy long-tipped cigarettes from the village shop, light them, take a few puffs and throw them away, into the stream, laughing when they heard them hiss as they hit the water. Then they would light another, take a few puffs and watch as it hissed and floated down the stream. This, they thought, was how the white man smoked his cigarettes.

Everyone knew that Jalib would go to *Wallait*. This used to fill him with pride. One day soon, he would think, he would be wandering the streets paved with gold. All the older boys dreamt of being taken out of the poverty of the village. They would burn with jealousy when they saw that the children of those who had gone to England were dressed in new clothes and had money to spend on whatever they wanted. They would talk for long periods of time about how pretty the *maims* were. They thought that *maims* were like *hoors* who spent most of their time wandering around in paradise; far from the existence of women from the village, who sold milk, eggs or other produce, when there was any. Their clothes bore the marks of their poverty; their faces were burnt by the scorching rays of the summer sun.

Jalib's early image of England was inspired by these older boys from the village. Whenever he sat with them, he listened intently to their descriptions of England and the riches it could give. They were awakened from their reveries at regular intervals as a train went past, puffing out clouds of steam and smoke. As it passed, they were silent, contemplating this example of the wonders of the white man. None of them had been on a train, except in their dreams. It always passed on into the distance, twisting through the hills as though in pain. The place to which the train took its occupants, who could be seen hanging on its sides, must be rich, they would think. When the train had passed, they would be alone again, to wait for the time when they could be white men.

'You couldn't spare a few pennies for an old man could you, son?' Jalib was shaken from his thoughts by a local alcoholic. When he had first seen beggars in England he had not believed they were real *goras*. He ran past the man without answering. His father had told him that these people were bad. They were dirty. Jalib could not believe they were white.

He turned fearfully into his street. He passed the shop from which his family bought their meat. The shopkeeper was from the same district as Jalib. Every time he went in there, the shopkeeper would tell him about his father and what good friends they were and that they had been in the same regiment in the army back home. The shop was not like those owned by the English people. Here everything was sold. Meat, sweets, spice, *dahl*, almost everything you would possibly need. Just like the big shops back home.

'What have you been up to, son?' On seeing Jalib, the shop-keeper had walked to the front of his shop. He was a big man. He had been here for a long time. Everyone came to him for advice because he was just about the only one in Jalib's street who spoke English. He stopped Jalib and lifted the boy's head to look at the marks on his face. Jalib remained silent, petrified.

'We haven't come here to fight . . .' the shopkeeper said sternly. Jalib pulled himself free and walked towards his own front door.

He knocked on the door, tears in his eyes. His father came and stood in front of him, towering over him like a giant. He was a tall man, slim, and he looked much older than he was. Jalib looked at his father; his body began to shake with fear.

'Have you been fighting again?'

Jalib bowed his head, his tears falling on the dry step like the monsoon rains on hard earth. His father grabbed him by the collar and threw his small body inside. Jalib crashed into the bottom of the naked stairs – they were still uncarpeted – his head hitting the bottom step.

'*Mather choud!* I work like a donkey to bring you here, to bring you up, and all you do is fight at school!' His heavy hand landed on Jalib's face and drew back to strike again.

'Don't hit him again! For God's sake, don't hit him again!' Jalib's mother ran towards him. Jalib had huddled in a ball and was crying loudly. 'Can't you see he's bleeding?'

His father walked away, cursing Jalib as he went into the sitting-room. His mother carefully raised her son's head and

20

wiped his tears. With her *dupatta* she started to wipe blood from Jalib's face. As she did this her heart beat fast, thinking it might be something serious. A sigh of relief went through her when she saw the blood came from Jalib's nose.

'Is it bad?' his father asked from the sitting-room.

'He's only a child. You shouldn't hit him like that. No, it's only a small cut. His nose, that's all.'

Jalib walked into the sitting-room. His father was sitting on their second-hand settee. Jalib remembered going with his father when they bought it. Jalib had seen many beautiful sofas and had told his father that he liked one he had seen in the window of a furniture shop in town. In that shop, things were set out neatly. Jalib told his father, with pride, where the shop was and what the man in the shop looked like. His father had stared at him and told him he was being silly, that they would not be able to afford anything from that shop for many years. He had patted Jalib lovingly on the back and then taken him to the second-hand shop where everything was piled on top of everything else. The difference between the two shops had left a deep mark on Jalib. His father had argued with the shopkeeper about the price of the settee and when he bought it and left the shop, Jalib remembered that his father had cursed the shopkeeper and called him a thief.

'Jalib, come here.' This was no longer the voice of the man who had struck him.

His mother had gone to the kitchen to make *roti*. His father always woke up just before Jalib returned from school and left for work a few hours later. He worked seven days a week.

'What happened? Who did you fight?' Jalib started to tremble again. He opened his mouth but nothing came out.

'*Gora* again?'

'*Ji,*' Jalib replied, bowing his head.

'Allah!' His father let out a sigh. 'Come here, son.' The smell of roasting chapattis was making Jalib's mouth water. The sound of his mother clapping the chapatti in her hands was heavenly music to his ears. The curry pan was letting its aroma escape. Jalib's thoughts were now on how soon he could get this ordeal over and sit down to eat. His father put his arm around him and said, 'You forget about fighting at school, Jalib, son. You'll be a man soon. Remember your auntie. Have you written to her lately?' Jalib shook his head.

'Do you know why you came here? We want you to be someone. A doctor, maybe. I work like a donkey. I never thought it would be like this. They say all sorts of things to us at work. We just take it. I know you must think we're cowards. But this is not our country. We've come here to work. It's a free country. You can do what you like. We've managed to buy this house. Some day we'll sell it and go back home. You're our only son. I want you to be someone.'

Jalib's thoughts went back to his village. Although he did not now think much about his friends and relatives back in Pakistan, when he first arrived he had missed the company of his friends and the stories they used to tell each other. Before his father came to Britain, he remembered the many times his parents would go without a full meal in order to fill his stomach. How, early in the morning, his mother would set off for the distant hill, returning at the end of the day with a bundle of grass for their only cow.

'Jalib, come and take this food up!' He ran free from his father's embrace and darted down the stairs into the cellar, leaving in his father's arms the thoughts he was having about Pakistan. 'Wash your hands before you touch the food! Don't they even teach you this at school?' his father shouted after him.

Jalib rushed through his food. His head was full of the coming battle. At least this time the whole school was involved in it. These thoughts filled him with a sense of confidence. At last he knew where he stood.

It had been a wet and cold winter morning when Jalib's plane touched down at Heathrow airport. His village was full of stories of how, when one got to the airport, the questions that were asked were so searching it was essential not to make a mistake. And if a mistake was made, no matter how trivial, then you would be returned to wherever you came from, on the next flight. So for weeks before he was due to leave Pakistan, Jalib had been drilled in the sort of questions the immigration officer would ask and what he should reply. He had often broken down and cried from the pressure of his training. His mother too had undergone the same sort of thing. His uncle had done most of the training as he had been to England, spoke English, and had been refused entry to the country.

'What is the name of your father? The full name, Jalib,' his uncle had asked him, over and over again. Jalib had been dazzled by these questions. He could not understand why he should have to be asked these silly questions: he knew the name of his father. So did everyone else.

'When were you born?'

How did he know? Jalib had asked his uncle, who had abruptly hit him. When he arrived in England, he was told, no matter how young he was, so long as he could talk, he was expected to answer every question he was asked. Through tears he had replied that even his mother didn't know the exact date of his birth so how could he? They had chosen a date that he could remember easily, and had written it in the documents too.

No sooner had his plane touched down than he was filled with terror. Perhaps he would make a mistake and never see his father again. Maybe they would not allow his mother into the country. From Islamabad airport the plane had flown into the skies filled with sorrow and pain. The passengers were overwhelmed by an avalanche of sadness, as their loved ones were left far behind.

Soft snow decorated the runways; sparkling snow-flakes drifted down from the skies. Walking down from the plane, Jalib had been convinced that the airport pavements were indeed gold, for the sun had been shining extravagantly. From fear and apprehension, his heart had beat fast against his chest. He had clutched his mother's hand tightly so that no one could take him away. His apprehension had bounced out of his chest and down the stairs.

The tension of the people who had just entered the airport and were about to be interrogated by unscrupulous immigration officers, seemed to suggest that they had arrived at their day of judgement. Their lives hung in a balance and depended on the whim of an immigration officer. One simple little mistake was enough for their dream to end and a nightmare to take its place. Everyone was aware that any one of them could be sitting on the next plane to Pakistan, refused entry and sent back amidst humiliating smiles.

Looking around the unfamiliar scene, Jalib wanted to break off a few slabs of this gold paving and go back to Pakistan. He

23

could not understand why he was having to go through all this fear in order to join his father.

The immigration officer started to ask Jalib questions in Punjabi! Jalib felt that there was no end to the power of the *goras*. They could even talk his language as though it was their own.

A massive sigh of relief had filled him as he ran into the arms of his father, who had been waiting nervously outside.

Jalib had often joked with his school-friends about their earlier experiences, what they had thought about England and what they had found when they arrived. One day Jalib had been just another peasant child. A fortunate one, as his father had gone abroad and his family's immediate poverty had gone with him. Suddenly he found himself part of a system which told him that he was a wog and that he must assimilate into a new way of life and forget his 'backward' ways. At the same time, that system ensured that the education he received wouldn't come in the classroom but in the playground.

At break, they often would laugh hysterically among themselves at the *goras'* stupidity, remembering that when they had first arrived at their junior schools the white children, who had never seen before anyone with a different coloured skin, had pulled their ears, thinking they weren't real. There were many times when white children at Jalib's junior school had tried to rub off his skin, convinced that his skin was dark because he did not wash.

The memories of his arrival and initiation into Britain came to Jalib in his dreams. He would wake up in a sweat as he saw himself flying away from his father in the arms of his sobbing mother. He dreamed he had said they owned two cows instead of, as his uncle had told him to say, one cow and a calf. Sometimes he would talk about such things with other children, but all of them kept some painful memories quiet. They even distrusted each other. Their parents had told them not to discuss themselves and their families with anyone because the police might come and take them away.

Shortly after his arrival in Britain Jalib had asked his father why, if there was so much gold on the streets, they didn't just take a few slabs and go back to Pakistan. His father had smiled and told him that stories of gold on the streets were just a *chakkar*. There was no gold, only long nights. Jalib should work hard, he said, and become a doctor, or something like that. Then his father could return to Pakistan while Jalib sent him money.

Jalib fought hard to sleep that night but he was haunted by the coming day and its dangers. The memories of his first fight with a *gora* were still fresh in his mind. When he first arrived in Britain, he had imagined that these *goras* were not real human beings but some sort of supermen. Especially when the immigration officer at the airport had questioned him in Punjabi, he had been convinced that there was no limit to their power. From then on he had lived under the impression that the children of the whites must also be all-powerful. Whenever he had been struck or abused, he had never managed to find enough courage in himself to retaliate.

But one day a white kid had hit him and without thinking much, except that he had had enough, Jalib had struck back in anger. His punch had landed on the nose of the white boy. On seeing a small stream of blood, Jalib had been filled with both fear and wonder: fear, because he was scared that this all-powerful white boy would release his implacable wrath on Jalib and that he could do nothing to save his skin; wonder, because he had never imagined that the blood of white people was the same colour as his own. When he had seen the white boy cry, he had jubilantly laughed, for he realized that the white boy felt pain as he did and did not like it, as he didn't. These memories were just about all he had left of the junior school. All the rest had faded into obscurity. For this was indeed the major lesson he had learnt from his early schooling.

Chapter 3

Next morning, Jalib's apprehensions melted when he saw his friends waiting in the bus queue. Almost everyone was carrying a big parcel. Hidden in his satchel, Jalib carried a poker.

'What you got there, Ranjit?' he asked, indicating the large paper bag his friend carried.

'The *goras* don't like *mirchan*. So I think we should give them some.'

Jalib smiled at Ranjit then. Holding hands, they boarded the bus. Summer term was nearing its end. Usually the children would be singing and dancing to their classrooms, but not today. Everyone in the school knew that trouble was brewing.

Jalib, Ranjit and Mohan were told the Headmaster would see them later. After assembly there was a staff meeting and the Headmaster suggested that school should be suspended because of the tense atmosphere. But after a long discussion with his staff this was decided against. The teachers considered the tension between the black and the white children was a natural part of school life. They agreed to be extra alert to catch troublemakers before they could do any damage. As the Headmaster left the room the teachers were already talking about where they were going to get their annual suntan when term was over.

At break the prefects stood near the school entrance keeping a wary eye on the children. 'Look! All the wogs are getting together. We got to show these black bastards that they can't come to our school and act as though they are still in their jungle! Any of the English kids don't come with us – well then, they are not on our side. So they going to get it like the wogs.' Big Jim was firmly in control of the white children. They shared his feelings; there was no dissension in their ranks. The demarcation lines were clear: in one corner of the playground stood all the black children, blanketed in nervousness; in the other, an arrogant mass of white children proudly showed their strength.

'Those wogs, do they have knives on them?' a small boy asked

26

Jim. The white children remembered stories their parents had told them that the blacks were a violent people and that they carried knives and did not wash. The comics they liked so much told these children that the people from the east, where their present antagonists came from, were really inferior, humble and subservient, and that it was important that white people were firm with them in order to keep them in their place.

'Some of me friends will come at dinner-time. We'll sort out these shit heads, our kid. They don't carry no knives. Last time they lied to me.'

An eternity passed before the signal for the end of break came. The tension melted into the serene calm of the countryside surrounding the school. The cows lifted their heads curiously, then continued feeding.

Weapons had been stored in desks. None of the teachers had caught anyone for possessing them, luckily. The bag full of chilli powder was the most prized weapon of all. Ranjit thought that as the whites always went around saying that the Asian children smelled of curry and garlic, why not let them have a taste of something really hot!

Not a single child at the school paid a blind bit of notice to the lessons after break. From some classrooms, those in which the white kids had their lessons, radiated an ugly hatred. It crawled menacingly along the corridors. From the classrooms in which the Asian kids were being taught the justifications of British society, a seething anger radiated, a resentment of the continued harassment at school and of the total indifference of the staff to their history and culture.

The dinner bell rang. Usually the children, driven by hunger, would rush towards the dinner hall. Today, the dinner hall was deserted. Hunger had subsided in the knowledge of the coming battle and the lessons it would teach. The teachers knew that something had overtaken the school. Some went unperturbed into the staff-room and shut themselves away from whatever was happening outside, thinking that their job was to teach, and then only when in class. What happened elsewhere was nothing to do with them! Others moved around the school corridors with an air of importance, but would not dare to venture beyond the safety of the school building. Outside was an alien environment, one they worked to maintain, bolster and create, but one from which, right now, they wanted to distance themselves.

The sun shone over the playground, in its full and warm beauty. The calm scenery was beginning to shake off its humility. The cows had moved closer to the playground and were looking across to it, as though they understood what was brewing in the air.

The Asian kids massed at the bottom end of a slope which cut neatly between the two playgrounds. When the school had first been built, each of the playgrounds had been surrounded by a protective wire cage. As a result of successive fights between the black and white children, however, the cages had been torn down, for whenever a fight developed the children formed a large circle around the fighters, and someone would climb on the wire to get a better view of the battle. Then someone else would join him . . . then someone else. Finally the weight of the children would bring down that portion of the fence and by the time a teacher arrived to break up the fight, the damage had been done – both to one of the fighters (invariably the black child) and to the netting.

Jalib looked across at the increasing mass of white children who were getting together at the top end of the hill, in the shadow of their derelict, redundant church.

'Where the hell did all that lot come from?' Ranjit had come closer to Jalib. The rest of the Asian kids moved about in an uneasy manner.

'I suppose they must have been at school all the time . . .' Jalib looked up at nearly a thousand white children. Some of them were singing obscenities at the black children.

The wind began to blow, mischievously changing direction every so often. The dinner ladies had come out to the playground to find out why none of the children had come for dinner. An awful sight met their eyes: on one side of the school nearly a thousand white children, on the other, three hundred Asians. The dinner ladies ran back into the school as a roar emanated from the white children. The prefects stood in the middle of the playground. The teachers peeped out of the classroom windows.

'Well, *yaroo*! Looks like we're going to get a hammering here!' Jalib shouted to a nervous and frightened mass of Asian children, none of whom could understand where so many whites had come from.

'You okay, Mohan?' asked Jalib. A feeling of a lost battle was beginning to overtake their camp, even before the battle had

28

begun. 'Don't think every one of our lads is going to stay in place, Jalib,' Mohan replied, as he saw some children trying to walk towards the rear of their gathering.

'Those that stay, stay. You going to stay, then?'

' 'Course!'

The whites charged. A few of the Asian kids ran away as they saw a powerful stampede rush towards them. Ranjit threw a handful of chilli powder into the air, then another. The wind had changed direction and it fell harmlessly to the side. He threw another handful at some approaching whites.

Jalib felt a sharp pain in his back as he was hit. Falling, he struck out at someone. He felt a foot tread on him, then someone tripped over him and fell. He put his hands to his head to avoid another blow there. All around him a pitched battle had started. Someone screamed as he was hit by a stone. The teachers ran towards the last few white children who had not yet reached their target.

'There you are, you dirty black git!' Big Jim ran towards Jalib, who had managed to raise himself off the ground. Jalib quickly pulled out the poker he had hidden down his trousers and struck Jim across the shoulders. Jim screamed. The stampede of the white children ran clean through the Asian kids, some of whom were nursing their injuries, consoled by the knowledge that at least they had braved the odds against them.

Where the white kids had assembled, the teachers now congregated. The Headmaster took command and led a charge at the remaining few children. The armies dissolved. The children were spread out in clusters in different parts of the area.

'That will be all for today! I want everyone in the assembly hall,' the Headmaster said to one of the teachers. 'I phoned the police and I think they will be here soon.' As he turned to go back towards the school, he commented, 'I think it would be a good idea if we kept the Asians separate until the police arrive. We don't want anything else to happen.'

The cows had moved into the far corner of the field. They had almost stampeded in fear of the noise of the screaming children. From a safe distance, they looked back at the wonders of modern education.

When the dust from the battle had settled, the whole play area was seen to be littered with a great assortment of weaponry.

While the children were herded into their assembly hall, the teachers slowly moved across the playgrounds, picking up the tools of the day's battle, in amazement.

'Some of you could have been seriously injured.' The police officer talked down to the children. The black children stood on one side of the assembly hall, the white children on the other side. Until the police arrived, the Asian children had been kept waiting in the gymnasium and all had been searched thoroughly. However, the search had not yielded anything.

'Look at these things!' The police officer pointed to a massive collection of weapons. Knives, pokers, chair legs, and many other things with which both sides had armed themselves. 'There is enough here to equip an army!'

'You lads are no longer in a jungle.' The police officer looked across the heads of the Asian children. 'This is a civilized country. I am not just blaming you, but you must learn to accept the ways of this country. This is a free country. Soon you will be leaving school and going into jobs and a life outside. Is this what you want to learn? How to fight?'

Jalib felt an anger towards the police officer, whose uniform was decorated with the signs of authority. The Headmaster had said much the same things as he was saying. Why didn't he understand that the fights on the playground were a part of the schooling? In fact, they were the school. Everything else was a supplement to those lessons.

'You children should really know better.' The police officer now looked across to the white children. He spoke over their heads. 'I'm not going to blame any one of you, but you have come to school to learn. You must show yourselves as an example to these people. You must show them the virtues of the British.'

Jalib smiled at these last comments. He felt that the white children were indeed showing them what the virtues of this country were! The police officer continued to talk, now to the blacks, now to the whites. No one really took any notice of him. He was not going to have to go back into the playground. In some respects, the presence of the police united the children. But the wounds of the battle were too fresh for the unity to surface.

After the police officer had spoken, the Headmaster assumed command. He was filled with fear in case he lost his job for not maintaining discipline in his school. He told the assembly that until the end of term the Asian children would be leaving school half an hour before the white children, and that arrangements would be made to minimize the chances of another battle erupting.

'Why can't you be like your parents?' He concluded his talk by looking in the direction of the Asian children. 'You have a chance of a better life. Look how your parents work. I will be contacting them to tell them in plain language what you are all up to in school.' At this point, he moved off the platform and went towards his office, with a business-like air.

'Jesus Christ our Lord tells us to turn the other cheek.' The R E teacher started to preach passivity. No one paid any attention to him either. But he continued to preach, hoping that perhaps these strangers to Christianity would see the light. No one did.

In town, at the end of the day, one of Jalib's friends from another comprehensive school told him that there had been a lot of trouble at his school as well, and that *goras* who did not attend the school had been involved in the fighting. Jalib recounted the events of the day at his own school.

'Well, if they are ganging up on us, we will have to come to your school as well.'

Jalib felt very bitter. The white children, who were already numerically stronger, had brought in friends from outside to help them in the battle. In the following weeks, almost all of Jalib's friends went to other schools to join with children who were similarly caught in the grips of racial terror.

On his way home that afternoon, however, Jalib braced himself for the now-familiar beating. He was beginning to think that it was just another part of his schooling.

Chapter 4

A blanket of rain covered the centre of town. Here and there umbrellas had been brought out. A line of people, heads bowed to avoid the rain, moved in and out of the Employment Office. The cars, whizzing past, threw up dirty water at them. Young people ran around as though their budding energy, even when it had no useful role in the productive machinery of a destructive society, would explode them.

Mohan stood in a line that moved, snake-like, around the building, its numbers forever increasing, everyone pushing close to the wall for shelter. Looking around him, he saw the distraught faces of the idle. From some radiated anger as they signed their living days away. Others seemed to accept their lot, as though making their mark each day at the Employment Office was the work of divine providence.

'Hey, John!' shouted Mohan to an old school-friend. 'What's the hurry, our kid? You got summat special to do today?'

'Yeah. I'm going home to go back to sleep. Skint, man! Might as well sleep until the dole arrives,' replied John as he walked towards the centre of town.

Mohan laughed, thinking of the times he too had felt too tired to struggle against the approaching day, its lures, its urges to spend, spend, spend. The adverts in the shops screamed, 'Save, Save, Save . . . with every pound you spend.' Their hypocrisy always left Mohan bemused; save money by spending it – how, when you don't have any in the first place?

Mohan made his mark and ran back out into the rain, pushing against a wall of human bodies.

Near by, the West Yorkshire Metropolitan Police station stood like an Orwellian Ministry of Justice. On its roof, tentacles stretched towards the heavens, listening and prying into the movements of the people. All in the name of freedom and democracy. Through its thick dark plate glass, the occupants could look and see anyone approaching from any direction. Beside it,

32

the Magistrates' Court, a small, flat building, seemed subservient. Towering over the Court, the fortress of the police headquarters was designed as if to show who were the real arbiters of justice. And, hidden from the eyes of the people, joining the two buildings, was an umbilical cord.

Surrounding buildings showed characteristics of anarchic planning. The offices of the local authority were housed in a tall building next to the Job Centre, into which expectant thousands poured daily. Offices all around contained faceless bureaucrats who strangled with red tape the society they pretended to help run smoothly.

Next to a virginal theatre, one of Poulson's monstrosities, stood Bradford Central Library, a palace of learning for students. Eight storeys high, containing books in almost every language and about every subject, it provided shelter for many of the local down-and-outs. Youth, especially Asian youth, also gathered on the second floor where the cafeteria offered sanctuary. Here the down-and-outs sat all day with their cold tea, observing with sorrowful eyes the downhill slide of youth.

Mohan had been looking through the 'Vacancies' column of the local newspaper.

'Not much here again,' he said to Jalib, who had been sitting in the café for a few hours before Mohan arrived. 'There's a job going at the hospital for a porter. Think I'll apply for it. You never know. I might even get it,' he jested.

'So will thousands of others. Who's going to look at you?' Jalib was a bit sarcastic. He felt any discussion about jobs was futile.

'Got to keep looking. My father is on three days a week now and he gets bloody narky if he sees me sitting around.' Already he could see himself working at the hospital, pushing patients around from ward to ward. He put his hand in his pocket to feel his wage packet, as though he had already started working.

'Same here,' Jalib answered, in a low tone as he sat fidgeting with an empty packet of cigarettes. 'Same story everywhere.' He was filled with a sense of helplessness. 'Got any cigs in that emergency pocket of yours?' Mohan asked slyly, knowing that when Jalib was short of money he would hide some cigarettes in his pocket and place an empty packet on the table in front of him.

'No. Not even a dog-end today. Don't sign on until tomorrow.'
This meant that it would be three more days before he received
any money. Mohan went to another table, where a large group of
people sat. He 'borrowed' a cigarette and came back. It was
common practice that one would ask to be 'loaned' a cigarette,
knowing full well that it was not borrowing but sharing the small
wealth of poverty.

A heated debate began at the table where Mohan and Jalib sat.
Mumtaz, an old friend of Jalib's, had recently graduated from
university in London. He was the son of a local restaurant owner
and would talk endlessly about the amount of land they had back
in Pakistan. They had just built a new *kothi* in Islamabad.

'Yes, this is a free country. If you have intelligence you can go
to university, get a degree and better yourself,' Mumtaz said as
he moved his spectacles up his nose, indicating by his gesture that
he was somehow involved in a mission to enlighten his country-
men. 'The trouble with you is you don't want to help yourselves!'

None of the others liked him. Mumtaz made sure that everyone
knew that he regarded himself, and wanted to be regarded, as
belonging to the upper echelons of his community.

Mohan took no notice of the accusation Mumtaz had thrown
at his listeners from his great height. 'Free country!' Mohan
exploded. 'I can't think of anyone, in all the people I know, who
hasn't some relative who has been either kicked out or questioned
by the immigration pigs.'

As the battle hotted up all ears were focused on the debate.
There was an air of unity against Mumtaz.

'People are only kicked out because they break the law,' he
replied as though he was addressing a grand jury. 'It is precisely
because there are such elements in our community that life is
made so rough for the majority of our citizens, who are essentially
law-abiding.'

Jalib was unusually silent because he could not trust himself to
speak. Everyone in the room was listening – all the down-and-
outs near the window, with their cold tea, the students and
housewives. He thought with anger about his cousin Maqsood,
his mother's nephew, who was in hiding, in Jalib's house, living
in fear of the immigration police. On the one hand Jalib felt
proud, confident that his people could always outwit the immigration authorities. Whenever he heard on the news, or through

someone, that a new regulation had been brought in, he would joke with his friends that it wouldn't take long for someone to find a way round it. But he knew, in reality, that the noose was always getting tighter.

'What bloody law?' Mohan interjected. 'They keep changing it every day.'

'It is the right and privilege of Parliament, as the elected representatives of the people, to make laws,' Mumtaz continued in his most didactic fashion. 'Those laws have to be enforced. You have a right to make your opposition felt. If one wishes to come to Britain, however, one must go through the proper channels.' He felt confident that his university education and his use of words would be sufficient for him to win this argument. But whenever he said anything about immigration, he was always very careful not to mention that the police could arrest any black person, on suspicion alone, and could hold them in prison indefinitely, without the right of trial. He always omitted this, for he was somewhat apprehensive that the Asians might get angry and vent their anger on him.

Although Jalib knew his cousin Maqsood had come here illegally, he never thought of that as a crime. He thought it didn't matter how anyone got here, as the doors to Britain had long since closed.

A voice from the crowd menacingly surrounding Mumtaz echoed Jalib's thoughts. 'The doors are closed, man! they don't like wogs and niggers – you one, you know.'

There was spontaneous laughter, which ended as quickly as it started. Mumtaz felt uneasy at the association.

'Of course it is difficult. But you must appreciate that the economy is in a bad way. This is a small island.' Mumtaz tried to bring in everything he had heard used as an excuse for keeping blacks out of Britain.

'So what we care?' The same voice again. 'I ain't made this mess!'

Mumtaz was becoming increasingly uneasy. He did not want to personalize the issue. He thought that he, himself, had after all managed to succeed in the rat race. He had obtained an honours degree.

'What I'm saying is, there is sufficient security in this country, for those of us who are here, to further ourselves, educate ourselves, get respectability . . .'

'Only security I'm used to is social security!' Mohan's comment was met with a roar of laughter. 'Now what do you make of that, sir?' Mohan asked sarcastically.

'You should get a job.' Mumtaz was on the defensive.

Jalib butted in with the voice of an interrogator. 'Where? Will your Buddha give me one? Or maybe you'll let me work in your *marabaas* in Pakistan.'

'It's gits like you I can't stand,' Mohan said, pointing a finger angrily at Mumtaz. 'Always talking fancy words. What do you know about us? The *goras* are shitting on us all over the place. The cops beat us up. There ain't no jobs, man! They don't want us no more!'

'Really.' Mumtaz felt a fear from the now-hidden, now-open threats that were directed at him. 'If you don't like it here, if it is so bad, why don't you go back? It's people like you that cause so much trouble. The British police are just about the best in the world. I've never had any trouble from the *goras* as you call them.'

'I bet you haven't!' Jalib ridiculed Mumtaz for the cowardice he showed and represented. 'Keep on licking, man!'

'It's pointless me wasting my time on rabble like you,' Mumtaz said, sensing that for all his education he was unable to explain the merits of the British system. He stood up and walked out. The group of youths who had gathered around the table dispersed, some cursing him, others thinking that perhaps there was some truth in what he said. But nowhere could they find any semblance of that truth in their lives. They went back to various tables. A few middle-aged white women had listened intently to the debate. They felt sympathy for Mumtaz and resented the others for not listening to such an intelligent person. As soon as the argument was over, these women returned to their tea and biscuits, pretending they had heard nothing.

The day wore on slowly. An endless stream of unemployed youth came and went, now sitting, now standing in the corridors or, if they had money, at the service counter. Some laboured through magazines, gazing at the wonders of civilization they could never afford. The occasional student, going through his or her notes, showed a sense of urgency.

'I got to go home, man,' said Mohan.

The monotony of the day was becoming unbearable to Jalib

too. The two friends left the library together, holding hands. The white people around always stared when they saw two blokes hand in hand.

The rain had become an unpleasant drizzle. They walked past the police station. Mohan spat at the walls.

A little while later, exhausted from the day's idleness, he sat with his eyes fixed to the television screen, watching an American detective film. As soon as one scene finished, he forgot it. Overlooking the gas fire were hanging pictures of Guru Nanak and Guru Gobind Singh. Guru Nanak looked serene and sagacious; Guru Gobind Singh smiled as he went into battle, an eagle on his arm and arrows across his back, towering proudly over his followers.

'Jagjit's windows were broken last night,' Mohan's mother said. She had finished her chores and come to sit in front of the television with her son. She talked above the strange scenes in a strange language flashing before her. 'About one o'clock in the morning.'

'Anyone hurt?' Mohan asked, forgetting the noise of gunfire that came from the television. He felt angry with himself for not knowing earlier.

'No. They just smashed the windows and ran away.'

Hardly a night went by without the sound of someone's windows breaking, followed by the sound of running feet. If the police were called, they generally came round the following day, wrote something down and went away.

'Did Jita know who they were?' Mohan asked, knowing the answer.

'No,' his mother sighed. 'They were shouting things before they smashed the windows, then they ran off.'

The police never traced the culprits.

Mohan heard his father moving around in the back room. Over the past three weeks, his father had been on short time and was usually in a bad mood. Mohan tried his best to keep out of his way.

'*Wahay Guru*,' his father said, as he entered the front room. 'Been looking for a job, son?'

'I went to the Job Centre this morning,' Mohan lied. He had stopped going there because it was pointless. 'I looked in the paper and there was nothing going.'

Mohan studied his father. Usually, when he questioned Mohan about his day's activities, it was in bitterness, as though his idleness was the result of laziness. Mohan was becoming apprehensive. He sensed a volcanic eruption was stirring in his father's questioning. He looked across to his mother, to see if he could detect the cause of this impending explosion. He became uncomfortable, sitting under the gaze of his parents. The reactions of his mother convinced him that trouble was brewing and he searched his mind to find what he had done wrong. Had someone seen him talking to girls? No! He dismissed this, for in the last few days he had been solely in the company of Jalib and his male friends. An urge was building in him to get up and run out of the house. His father sensed Mohan's apprehension.

'I found something on your table this morning,' his father said. He was ready to attack now.

Now Mohan knew what it was all about. Terror ran through his spine. He cursed his own carelessness. He had been late signing on this morning and had left the house in a rush.

'*Haram zada!*' His father's fury was now out in the open. 'This is what I found!' He threw the packet of cigarettes directly at Mohan's face. Mohan froze. The packet hit him smack in the face. His body stiffened. He felt shame, sorrow and fear run through him. He looked across at his mother, who returned a stone cold glance.

'How long have you been smoking?' His father roared. The frustration of his short-time work, his family obligations, a sense of loss of honour and of loss of pride in his son because of his sacrilegious act, burnt into him. Mohan lowered his head. He did not answer. There was no answer. He had hidden this fact from his father for years. In order to disguise the smell of tobacco, before he came home he always chewed mints, and as soon as he came home he always cleaned his teeth. A moment's carelessness had brought this monumental calamity upon him. He had not only broken a religious taboo, he had hurt his parents deeply. He felt ashamed.

'Look at me, you no good *harami*!' His father stood up. Mohan felt like curling up. He knew there would be no escape. C R A C K ! The side of his face burned with pain. S M A C K ! He could hear his father's voice cursing him between blows. He heard his brothers and sisters stir upstairs. But he knew none of them would dare come down. He lost count of the blows and curses.

'Get up and get out of this house! And take this filth out of the house with you!' His father walked out of the room, flushed with shame and anger. Mohan picked himself off the floor, tears rolling down his cheeks. He stole a look at his mother. She seemed cold and hostile, as earlier. Sobbing, he put on his coat. As he opened the door to leave, his mother came up behind him. 'I'll leave the back door open. Come back after your father has gone to sleep,' she said affectionately. 'Why did you bring this filth into our house?'

Mohan slowly closed the door and walked out into the darkness. He felt like crushing the remaining cigarettes but knew they would provide a welcome companionship in this hostile night. He lit one as he walked and thought that he would have to convince his parents he had stopped smoking.

Chapter 5

'They came to our house,' Jalib said, putting his hand in his pocket to look for his cigarettes, 'at seven o'clock this morning. Bastards! Knocked me down, ran around the house, turned everything over. My little sister was crying.' He lit a cigarette. His body was shaking with anger and frustration. He looked from face to face, all familiar faces. 'Sit down, *yaar*,' he heard a voice say. In his anger, he had forgotten he was still standing. As he pulled up a chair, he looked around the café as though he had never been there before. Plain walls, punctuated here and there by curry stains where drunks had written their names with the sauce. An old, dirty chandelier hung from the ceiling. A cat lay in deep sleep in front of the gas fire. A juke box in the corner played an old Lata song.

He recounted the story of how, early that morning, the police had raided his house – about twenty policemen in all. The plain-clothed policemen had knocked loudly on his door. His mother had shouted to him to go and see who they were. As he opened the door, they had burst past him. After searching the house and taking everyone's name, they had gone out with a lot of letters and all the passports. They had come, they told him, looking for his cousin. He had looked out and seen that Shaheen, across the road, was looking through her curtains. The whole street had been blocked by Panda cars.

'You'd think it was Starsky and Hutch. So many pigs to catch a bloody mouse like our Maqsood. You should have seen them, everywhere, walkie talkies burbling out all the time.' The events of the morning were still running through Jalib's mind. So much force, he thought, to catch one little man.

'Did they get him?' asked Mohan.

'Did they hell! He had just gone out to the shop. He'll be shitting himself now, though,' Jalib replied, and they burst out laughing.

'Hey, General!' Mohan shouted to the waiter. A lame young

man, who had worked in the café for as long as anyone could remember, came. 'Give our kid a cup of char, will you?'

General got his name from the stories he told about his father who, he insisted, had been a general in the British army during the Raj. No one believed him, but no one called him a liar. General, fitting well into the rundown surroundings of this part of the city, walked to the table at which Jalib and his friends were sitting, placed the tea on it and said, 'They came, friend, you okay?' No one took any notice of him and he was used to it now. He wiped the table, picked up the ashtray and walked by into the kitchen.

The owner of the café looked on, with accusing eyes. 'Vagabonds,' he thought. 'No good for anything. Lazy bastards, their parents think they're out looking for work.' He cursed them for being idle. He had tried once or twice in the past to bar them from his café but they had reacted violently. He would have called the police, but they provided some income during the day. Most of his customers were white and they came only after the pubs had shut. They were much better customers, he thought; they didn't fuss like his own people. 'They'll never change,' he said to himself, 'always moaning, won't help themselves. They always want to have everything laid on for them.'

He had overheard the conversation between Jalib and his friends. These illegal immigrants made life difficult for decent people like himself, he thought. There are, after all, too many of us here, and the more people that come the worse it is for the rest of us. He had seen that, over the years, his white customers had become increasingly prone to swearing racist abuse at him. He always smiled at them because he knew they would be paying him.

With concern in his voice, he shouted over to Jalib, 'They came for Maqsood, son? Things are getting bad for us folks here, aren't they?'

'What you care?' Mohan shouted back. 'You too busy making money to care what happens to us folks.' The owner didn't answer. He turned his head to his books and began studying how his business was progressing.

Only Jalib and Mohan were left now in the café. They sat in silence for a while, listening to an old Lata love song.

Jalib could still hear his sister screaming, see his mother huddled in the corner of the front room, too scared to move as

41

the police ransacked her house. After they left, she sat down near the front door and cried. The tears of his mother filled Jalib with hatred for the police.

'You remember when your uncle got kicked out?' he asked Mohan. 'Did your family not care? No, I mean, didn't they say anything?'

Jalib was angry with his father for the way he had accepted the raid as part of the natural order of things. His father was fond of saying, like Mumtaz yesterday, that this was a free country.

Mohan looked disturbed. He did not like talking about his uncle who had been deported from Britain. 'They kept quiet,' he admitted. 'Nobody said anything.' He remembered how his father had sat in silence when he heard the news of his brother's arrest. 'Everyone was shocked and scared,' he told Jalib. A solicitor had explained to his father that a person could not appeal against the Home Office decision until he had actually been deported. The solicitor had asked for £500. He said that even after the appeal had been lodged in India, it would take years to be heard.

Mohan sank into Jalib's mood of despair. What could either of them do about anything? 'For six years my granny's been trying to come to live with us,' he said. 'There are always papers and interviews . . .'

'Cut it out, Mo,' Jalib butted in. 'These things get me down. Let's talk about something else.'

'Yeah, let's talk about something else.'

There was silence, but for the love song which was still playing. Mohan stood up. 'I've got to go soon. Have to do some shopping for mum.'

Jalib shook his head at him, his mind still troubled with thoughts of Maqsood.

'See you later then.' Mohan walked out, the door closing slowly behind him. They never fixed a time or place to meet up. Sooner or later, as they wandered aimlessly from place to place, they would meet. Jalib, after paying for his tea, walked out of the café.

Back streets of Manningham. Derelict houses. Where once long streets had been full of life, now rubble and heaps of rubbish. Here and there were houses in which a family still lived. Mostly, the area was deserted.

The lack of traffic had made the rubble a haven for young

children. They were dotted around in large clusters. Playing *guli danda*. Oblivious to the history of the streets in which they now played. Colourful *salwars* and *kurtas*, softly lifted by the cold breeze of the approaching evening. Above the noise of the children, a mother was shouting for a child to come home. The children, as though nothing existed apart from their games, continued unperturbed.

A group of children had trapped a cat in an overturned drum, which had become a part of this landscape. They were shouting '*billi, billi, billi*'. When they had been babies, their parents had told them horrific tales about evil cats and how they would scratch out the eyes of a child who did not behave and listen to his parents. Now they had a collective strength from their numbers and were teasing the cat. 'Come on then, *billi, billi, billi*.' The rest of the children, on learning that some new game had been discovered, ran and crowded around the drum.

Terrified, the cat clawed into the metallic sides of the drum. There was no escape. It was doomed. Some of the children turned the drum on its top so that they could see the cat at the bottom and so that it could not escape. They began to throw stones at it. Each time the cat would give out an eerie, shrill cry, at which the children got more excited.

Jalib walked past, his head full of the morning's events. He glanced over his shoulder, disturbed by the noise of the children. 'What have you got in there?' he shouted. '*Billi ji*,' answered a boy, jumping up and down with excitement.

Jalib walked over to them. The children descended to total silence, scared by the presence of an older person and worried about the possible consequences. Jalib looked into the drum. The cat was breathing heavily, blood oozing from its mouth. He thought of Maqsood, shook his head and walked on. By now the children had dispersed and only the death cries of the cat could be heard. The children had all fled to their homes.

Without thinking where he was going, Jalib stood in front of a pet shop. In the window was a picture of a middle-aged white woman, smiling, serene, kind, compassionate, embracing a lively cat. Underneath the picture was an advertisement for cat food. The shop window contained an assortment of pet foods, stuffed pigeons and cages. He gazed into the eyes of the cat and thought of the one he had left dying in Manningham's dying streets. 'Here she is cuddling a cat when my cousin is being hunted like an animal. Waiting to be caged and then kicked out by a society which no longer needs his labour,' he thought. The picture of the woman and the cat was a reflection of the reality in which he was trapped. 'A society,' he thought, 'not fit for humanity.' How could people like her think so much about cats when so many of his people were living in such fear?

All around people were rushing. Some to work, others going home. A small group of white youths were running. 'Cops, I bet,' Jalib thought. He had been tempted to run with them. 'Must be up to something nice!' Then his gaze returned to the pet shop picture. He felt an urge to smash the window. Perhaps he could smash the fetters that bound him to this life. Perhaps this would break the invisible chains which meant that Maqsood would be on the run for ever, until he was finally caught. There were too many people around. He pushed these thoughts out of his head. He looked back in the direction from which the youths had come. A police car was flashing its beacon. The youths had disappeared and Jalib jumped on an approaching bus.

Chapter 6

'You said you would come straight home, son,' his mother said as she combed his sister's long black hair.

Jalib looked at his sister. It was difficult to believe she could be so calm now. This morning she had been screaming with fear as her home was invaded, like a scene from television come to life. He looked at her eyes. She must have struggled when her mother put *kala* on them. Four years ago he had carried her into the house from the hospital. How quickly she had grown. Girls grow up much quicker, he thought. He had had a big fight with his family after her birth. He had wanted to distribute *ladoos* and sweets, as a thanksgiving to Allah for delivering his little sister, but his mother and father had shouted at him in disgust for having these thoughts. 'One does not celebrate the birth of a daughter,' his father had told him. 'Daughters are not like sons. Daughters, when grown, will go to someone else's house. They are passing strangers in this house.' Jalib had protested that he was happy to have a sister and that they should celebrate that Allah had given them such a beautiful and healthy girl. His father had cursed him for forgetting the old ways.

'I stopped to see some friends,' he explained to his mother. He had left the house earlier to call at the police station. 'They said they will send us a letter after they've finished their inquiries,' Jalib told her, bitterly.

'Will those men come back again tomorrow?' Nasreen asked. She felt safe now. They would not harm her. After all, they had not taken her away when they came. She had told her friends the story but they had teased her, saying she was lying.

'Don't you be worried, now. They won't come back again.' Jalib smiled and put his hand on his sister's head, which his mother smacked as she saw her artistic combing being roughed up.

'Good. I don't like them!' Nasreen looked up at her mother with pleading eyes.

'How long you going to comb her hair?' asked Jalib, the day's frustration now coming up in him in waves which he was having difficulty containing.

'I am hungry.' He sank into the sofa and looked out of the window.

'Your father will be up soon and you will have to wait until then,' his mother replied. 'Girls have to look pretty, you know,' she protested, as she continued to comb her daughter's hair.

'I suppose you have been loafing around, even when...' She wanted to talk about Maqsood but was frightened, in case she said something wrong. Her husband had told her many times that she must keep herself to her home and not get involved in anything else. She feared her husband. She did not understand how, when he was so gentle to her in Pakistan, he could be so cruel here. She had been a good wife. She did everything she could to keep the house organized and clean.

She looked across at her son who was looking out of the window. She amused herself with thoughts that he was thinking about Shaheen. He looked back at his mother, sensing that she had seen through him, turned over and started fidgeting with some records he had recently bought.

'I was thinking just now,' he lied, 'that maybe we should plant some roses in the front garden.'

'I bet you were!' She smiled at him, 'I know what you were thinking about. Shaheen's a woman now. She is very beautiful, isn't she,' she teased him.

'I wasn't thinking about her!' He got angry at his vulnerability to his mother.

'I've seen him sit here for ages, Mummy, looking over there,' Nasreen said innocently.

'Shut up or I'll break your stupid neck, you stupid little cow!' he shouted and walked out of the room.

'Don't swear at your sister, Jalib! She's only a guest here, you know,' his mother shouted after him as she continued to comb her daughter's hair. By now, Nasreen was getting irked over all the fussing about her.

Jalib returned with an apple. He sat down and began to munch it loudly, thereby reinforcing his protest that he was hungry.

'You'll just have to wait until your father wakes up,' his mother replied to his gesture.

'Will they catch Uncle Maqsood?' Nasreen asked Jalib. She

was very fond of Maqsood as, unlike Jalib, he never shouted at her. She always waited for Maqsood to come home from work or wherever he was, as he always brought her something.

'Don't you be thinking about your uncle Maqsood now.' Jalib cursed the police for making his sister think such things. She was too young to be thrown into the ugliness of their lives. By now, Nasreen had been set free by her mother and had jumped on to the sofa next to her brother. She was looking with interest at something in the street.

'Your father is awake now,' his mother commented, pressing her hands on her knees to support herself as she stood. Without saying anything else, she went out of the door and down the stairs into the kitchen.

Jalib noticed that his sister was looking at Shaheen. 'Go and play in the garden,' he ordered.

'I don't want to play,' she protested.

'Don't answer back! Go and play, I said,' he said in make-believe anger. She was too young to know his thoughts. She obediently walked out of the room and disappeared into the back garden.

Shaheen was standing in the doorway of her house. She was talking and laughing joyfully with a friend. Jalib felt a strange desire stir in him as he saw Shaheen laughing and joking, her *dupatta* dangling on her shoulders, her long black hair blowing in her face. Jalib began to imagine himself clearing her face of the blanket of hair. He imagined he was holding her and singing to her as those actors did in Indian films. He sat there, transfixed by her beauty, and slowly intoxicated himself with her existence. Hidden behind the veil of his curtains, he felt safe but guilty for spying on her. He was suddenly roused from his daydreaming by the sound of his father coughing as he walked down the stairs. Jalib turned round in fright and started to read the sleeve of a record. He would be beaten and humiliated if his father discovered him gazing with longing at Shaheen.

Unlike his mother, his father was ruthless and brutal to his children. 'When did you get back from the station?' his father asked, as he tried to rub the unnatural sleep from his eyes. He yawned as though to free his aching, ageing body from the night's burden. He never questioned his existence. He slept and worked. Since he had come to England he had never joked or played with his children. Like thousands of other workers from the Indian subcontinent, he had fitted into the mills of Bradford as though he had been destined for them.

'A few hours ago,' Jalib lied. He did not wish to have his father's wrath unleashed on himself. His father would not understand what had gone through his head, and why he had been out for most of the day, Jalib thought.

'Well, what did they say? Are they going to give the passports back or not?' His father questioned Jalib, trying to hide any signs of anger at the fact that the police had burst into his house in the early hours of the morning.

'They said they would write to us when they have finished their inquiries.' Jalib was upset by his father's apparently carefree attitude towards the morning's incident.

'Then they will. It's a free country. Maqsood has caused me so many problems ever since he set foot in this house.'

'Free country!' His father's words stung Jalib deeply. 'They come to our house. OUR HOUSE!' Jalib almost forgot that he was talking to his father. He had never raised his voice in his father's presence. 'They rampaged through everything and still it's a free country!' he said, cursing his father for being so placid. He looked into his father's face with disgust in his eyes. Still, he felt sorry for his father. He never went anywhere. He just slept and worked. 'Work' didn't mean anything to Jalib as he had had only two part-time jobs since he left school three years ago. Jalib felt a bit apprehensive about having raised his voice. His father might hit him for shouting at him.

'Ah, well. It's all in the hands of Allah. I did what I could for him. I can't keep on putting my family at risk for him for ever, you know, son,' his father said, with a deep sigh, which meant that he did not feel in a very argumentative mood. Jalib felt a cool and soothing breeze of relief go through his body. 'It's only because of your mother that I put up with him for so long.' He stopped and started to think how much his wife had cried when she heard that her nephew had finally arrived in England. He had not really objected to giving Maqsood sanctuary. Maqsood's father had given him some money towards his fare to England when he had first come. He thought that by harbouring Maqsood he would be able to pay back some of the debt that he owed Maqsood's father. That debt could not be valued in money terms alone. Also, the act would raise his prestige among the *biradari*. 'A man has to make his own way in life,' he thought, as he gazed at Jalib.

'You know where he'll go, don't you, father? Perhaps you could send him some money. He had hardly any when he left this morning.'

'Ask your mother to give you thirty pounds,' his father replied, thinking that this was a cheap price to pay to get rid of this problem and live in peace.

'What's he going to do with thirty pounds?' protested Jalib.

'Do you think money grows on trees? You should go out and get a job instead of loafing around all day, and then you'll understand how hard it is to earn money!'

These words were bitter to Jalib. He felt utter hatred towards his father.

Jalib's father had spent many years in the British army in Pakistan. Although he did not like to talk about it, the experience had given him a deep sense of acceptance of the way things were. Whenever he looked at Jalib, he was filled with confusion. He could not understand why his son had turned out as he had. Ever since he arrived in England, Jalib had done nothing but get into trouble with whites.

In Pakistan, Jalib's father had spent his life in misery, forever trying to make ends meet, always in debt to local money-lenders. In fact, he could not recall a day when he was not in debt.

The news had spread like wildfire throughout the district: they were looking for workers in Britain. It had been a hot summer's day. Jalib's father had been sitting in the shade of a tree with other men from the village, casually smoking a hookah. The beat of a drum bounced off the surrounding hills. At first they all thought it was just an advertisement for some *maila*. The beat came closer and closer. Then it stopped. Through a loudspeaker mounted on top of a *danga* a voice rang out:

'Go to Britain where the streets are paved with gold. Go to *Wallait*, *sajno* – the streets are paved with gold. *Choudhary* Newab of Jehlum is selling cheap visas . . .' the voice repeated itself over and over again, giving the same message. When the voice stopped, the drum started its joyous beating and passed on to the next village.

The men sat down again and for a moment all were silent. It was true, many people were making their way to Britain. Those who had some money had already left. Those who could just support themselves remained and tried frantically to raise the money to purchase a visa and a ticket to Britain.

'If only I had some money to buy a visa this poverty would be over,' Jalib's father had thought as he walked into the scorching heat of the midday sun. His mind travelled through the areas where he could get some money. The *choudhary*, like many others, was asking for five thousand rupees. It was an impossible amount for a poor peasant to raise.

That night, Jalib's father spent many hours talking to his wife about how they could raise money from within the *biradari*. He went through all the people in his *biradari* who owed him a favour from the past. They added up their total wealth. Jalib's mother's jewellery amounted to over one thousand rupees. She had carefully hidden it away so that she could spend it some day on the marriage of her children, especially if they had a daughter. This was the jewellery she had received at her own wedding. The cattle and goats would fetch another eight hundred or so rupees. After adding up all their wealth, Jalib's father sat back with a feeling of helplessness. All their wealth did not amount to enough to buy the visa and then there was the question of the ticket. The agents who sold the visas were insistent that the buyer of the visa should get a return ticket, and the return air ticket would have to be handed in to a person the agent would nominate in Britain. This ensured a double killing for them.

The days that followed crawled miserably by for Jalib's father. He had been running round to various relatives, raising a few hundred rupees here and a few hundred there. As not everyone from the family could go to Britain, it was generally agreed that Jalib's father should be the one to go and, once there, not only could he repay the debt but he could also get someone else over.

The day finally came when he had raised enough cash to pay all the costs of his trip. He travelled to Jehlum to see the agent, filled with anxiety lest someone should rob him, or even that the agent would disappear after receiving the money. It had happened to many people.

'May Allah help you,' the *choudhary* said, slyly, as he put the money in his pocket. 'It makes me feel good to see my people helping themselves.' Jalib's father thought, with hatred, that the *choudhary* was not really referring to anyone but himself. 'I will have the passport and all other papers ready for you as soon as possible. Make sure that you give the return ticket to my son.' Jalib's father had not said much, but nervously handed over the money and came home. He felt safer, learning that, as the *choudhary* was doing a thriving business selling visas, it was unlikely that he would disappear with his money.

The next few weeks, Jalib's father spent in tense anticipation, waiting the arrival of the *choudhary*'s man to tell him that all his papers were ready and that he would be leaving on the next plane for Britain. He had made many visits to Jehlum to check on progress. Finally, he was told that his papers were ready and he could travel within a few weeks.

For days before he was due to leave, he held Jalib tightly in his arms. He was filled with uncertainty and fear. He did not know how long it would take him to repay all his debt and save enough money to call his wife over.

But the question of when again he would be able to live with his wife and his son blurred into the background, in face of the present life. The last few days that he had before making the journey to Britain, Jalib's father spent mostly with his wife and son. Every night, his house would be full of well-wishers and people who would ask for him to try to get their son into Britain. For hours on end, he had to sit and talk to old friends, assuring them that he would not forget, that he would try his hardest to get his friends visas. He did not know how he would get visas, but he had not been able to find it in himself to refuse any of his friends or relatives. He understood that, for everyone else who could not afford the journey, he was a symbol of escape from their present miserable lives.

The last night he spent talking and joking with his wife, about all the times they had sweated under the merciless heat of the sun, to till the land with their ageing cattle and to water and wash the livestock.

'We've been poor, yes. But Allah has given us much more than many people,' Jalib's father had said on that cool starry night. His thoughts went to his friends who also tilled the land for some landlord but who, unlike him, did not even have their own cattle.

'We are still the fortunate ones – for at least we've been able to raise the money.'

His wife sat in silence most of the time, both happy and regretful. Happy, for she knew that the life they had lived for so long would now change forever. Sad, for she did not know, could not be sure that her husband would not leave her and forget her once he got to England. It had happened to some women she knew whose husbands had gone to England. They had not taken their wives with them or bothered to send for them. It further worried her that by the time he had repaid all the debt and saved enough for his family to go and join him, they might not be allowed in. But she pushed these thoughts quickly out of her mind. What really mattered was that they had found a way to escape their poverty.

'Why do you look so sad?' he asked her, 'I'm going to work for a few years and even if they don't allow you to come, I'll come back and we can make our life here.'

He did not sleep the night before his journey. Until the early hours of the morning, well-wishers had been there. One group would hardly have left before another would come to pay their respects and wish him a safe journey.

The morning sun came from beyond the hills as it always did. The dew had quickly evaporated. The whole village was full of excitement. Jalib did not really understand what was going on but he knew that he would not be seeing his father for a long time. Everything passed through his head in confusion. He thought about all the things he would be able to buy as soon as his father started to send money home.

Painfully but happily, his father had torn himself from his family and friends and set off on his journey to Britain. All the fears that he felt melted as he saw behind him the poverty that he was leaving. The whole village turned out to say farewell. A huge procession of people accompanied him to the point where a van was waiting to take him to the airport. As he entered the van, the villagers were silent.

The van moved off, up the rugged road. Jalib's father stole a last look in the direction of his wife and son. Jalib was clutching his mother's legs; she held her *dupatta* firmly in her teeth.

The journey by air was exciting. It was as though the whole plane was filled with a sense of wonder and triumph.

However, as Jalib's father did not know what to expect when he reached Britain, he was, like many before him, completely at the mercy of the agent's representatives.

'Don't worry, brother. You won't always have to live like this.' Jalib's father met one of his friends from Pakistan, a man he had known in the army, and moved into a room with him. Because Jalib's father worked the night shift and his friend worked in the day, they were able to share the same bed. One slept while the other worked. 'It's no good really looking for a place to buy, even after you've got enough money for a deposit, because the English people won't sell to us,' his friend would say, despondently.

'I can't think about a house yet. I'm still paying off debts. Allah has been kind to me. I've not fallen seriously ill and I've been able to put in lots of hours.' They would talk briefly and then one of them would leave for work.

For more than two long years, Jalib's father had hardly taken a single day off. There were many occasions when the overlooker or the manager would swear at him but, although he was seething with anger and resentment, he would reluctantly take everything for the sake of the debts he had incurred and the money he needed to bring his family here. That was his goal and everything else was secondary.

When he first arrived in Britain, he set his mind on the fact that he would try to return to Pakistan and see his family. But the cost of the journey and the loss of pay that it entailed meant that he could not do it. All around him, people talked about bringing their families to Britain and said if they intended to do it, they must do it soon, because there was talk that the government was thinking of stopping families of workers coming to live with them. Jalib's father had frantically tried to save money. If he could not get his family over before the new Act was passed, he would probably have to live apart from them for ever.

Looking across at Jalib, he knew his son had no knowledge of the tension and turmoil and pressure he had gone through to bring his family here. At that time he never imagined that his son would spend his youth in idleness on the dole.

His years of loneliness, the endless nights at the mill, the tension caused by the fear of losing his family, and the permanent pressure of his debt, had robbed him of all happiness and joy. Although he was now financially much more secure, many years of his life had melted into the machines at the mill.

Hunger rumbled in his belly and the clock on the wall told him that he had not long to go before he went to work. In fact, his body, accustomed to this routine, knew it without the assistance of a time-piece.

They ate their food in virtual silence. Only Nasreen was making the occasional childish comment. The others were all preoccupied with the events of the morning. The father was worried that the police might be back for further questioning. The mother was lost in deep thought about the situation of her nephew. She remembered how she had shed tears of happiness when she learned that Maqsood had finally reached England, after months of travelling round the world, believing that soon he would be able to live a bit more comfortably. And then, perhaps, her brother could come, too ... Jalib was caught between anger towards his father for showing no signs of caring for Maqsood, and a sense of his own helplessness. He didn't even know what, if anything, could be done to help Maqsood.

After finishing their dinner, Jalib poured out the tea and passed it over to his father, and then began helping his mother clear up. They always ate in the cellar. His father lit a cigarette and walked up the stairs, taking his tea with him, leaving behind him a trail of smoke which mingled with the smell of freshly cooked chapattis. Seeing his father smoke gave Jalib an urge to smoke but he knew he would have to wait until his father had gone to work. After putting the dirty plates in the sink, he followed his father up the stairs.

'Allah,' his father sighed as he put on his coat and picked up a bundle of food he would need for the night shift. He looked at his wife and then at his two children. Without further ado, he said, '*Khuda hafiz*,' and walked outside. As always, his work-mates were waiting outside his front door. He got into the car and Jalib watched it disappear around the corner. His mother had gone into the front room and was watching a documentary on the television.

'*Ammi-ji*, I'm going to the phone box. I won't be long,' Jalib lied as he excused himself and went out of the house to smoke a cigarette. As he left the house, he wondered what his mother made of all those things she saw on television. She didn't speak or understand any English. Without waiting for his mother's reply, he shut the door behind him. He knew what she would say, and left before she could.

He looked up at Shaheen's house. He could see the outline of her body moving about in her bedroom, behind the curtains. He saw that she was holding some sort of garment against herself. He felt a strange desire to be with her stir in himself. She came towards the window. He quickly moved on, in case she should see him spying on her.

Chapter 7

The early morning dew shone like pearls on the leaves that grew sporadically in and around the village. The soft *Azaan* of the village mullah was announcing the beginning of another day. The cockerels, from various parts of the village, loudly reinforced the mullah's call. Everyone understood this to be a holy sign, the cockerel's *Azaan*. Behind the hills to the east, the sun was waiting to reveal its implacable might and glory. Women with *tokras* full of dung were rushing to the fields or plots of land on which they and their menfolk worked. They hoped to get their chores done before the sun rose to its full, merciless glare.

She had sat and watched her son rush through his breakfast. He was eager to be with his friends. 'Take your father's *parna* with you,' she shouted to Jalib, 'and don't play in the sun too long.' She always ate after her son finished his food, especially in the morning. She loved to watch his little hands tearing the *paratha* and shoving it in his mouth. His eyes were so full of childish dreams and fantasies.

She sat in the small kitchen, patiently blowing into the fire, watching the wood burn under the *tawa*. She thought of her *pardesi* husband, far away in a strange land called *Wallait*. People said that white women were very beautiful and very free. She tortured herself with images of her husband wrapped in the arms of some *goree*. Surely these women were really *hooran*! That's what they must be, she thought, and that is why they were so carefree and happy. She knew that soon she would also be there, in *Wallait*. The thought filled her with terror. She would arrive, near by her husband would be waiting. She was aware that in order to reach him she would have to answer questions, many questions. Perhaps her answers would not be what they wanted to hear and then she would have to spend the rest of her life in this loneliness.

Almost every night after their work was done, the women of the village sat together. Jalib's mother always felt a strong sense of freedom as well as loneliness when she sat with the women. In the company of the women she would jest about her poverty and criticize the mullah, who had grown fat before her eyes while her family was forever struggling to make ends meet. The men were forbidden by custom to tread where the women gathered, so she didn't have to keep covering her head and looking down, as though by her existence she was an intruder. Among the women she could be herself, talk openly about anything that came to her lips, occasionally venturing to ridicule someone else's husband for not being manly.

The women shared in celebrating births of sons and marriages. Even grief could be shared and the death of a loved one made easier to bear. The loneliness of a life of poverty and drudgery would fade for a while. Those whose husbands had already gone to England would talk and laugh for many hours about this distant land, where their problems would be over. They would sing songs in praise of Allah for being so kind. Those not so fortunate sat in silence and quietly let the melody of their sad lives – the endless hours of work in the fields under a scorching sun – sing its eternal song. This was the song for the vast majority, but they shared in the happiness of those who were leaving the hell of poverty.

Many men had gone to England some years earlier. They were now sending for their wives and children.

'So you'll be joining your *khassum* soon!' Jalib's mother pretended not to hear the teasing voice. She had endured so much frustration for so many years.

'Forgotten what it feels like?' asked another woman. The rest were engulfed in laughter. Jalib's mother blushed and joined in the laughter.

Sometimes at night the emptiness of her house would become unbearable. She would wake Jalib, sit him on her lap and stroke his hair gently, telling him about England. Jalib was dazzled by the thought of streets of gold, a blanket of gold covering everything. This he always saw in his dreams after he had been talking with his mother about England. There were no beggars, she told him. None of the evil policemen would be there, like those who, whenever they came to the village, had to have great meals cooked for them, with his mother going hungry the next day. Jalib remembered how his father used to joke with the policemen, out of fear. On occasions his parents would argue for a long time after the policemen left because his father had been obliged to give them money. Jalib's mother would never tire of telling him how good life would be for them, once they got to England. Jalib would be comforted, never doubting her.

The day came when she told the women that she had received a letter from her husband and that she would be gone by the end of the month. The other women sat in silence and listened to every detail of what she said, and what her husband had told her about life in England. They had machines there which did cleaning, and by turning knobs you could sit back and the machine would cook the curry for you, her husband had written to her. The other women had listened with great interest, as though she had already been to England and had just returned with first-hand knowledge. She told them then that she was frightened of going in a plane. They all laughed. It was a fear which most of them never would experience.

She left her village in tears. Tears of happiness, for she would be joining her husband and her family would be together again after all the long years. Tears for her friends and relatives. Fear, sorrow and happiness overwhelmed her. Clutching her child close, in case he slipped away from her and was stranded here, she set off on her journey to a land that seemed like a distant Shangri-La.

Now she watched the television screen flash and talk to her. Sitting in front of the screen, her eyes transfixed, her mind would slip back to the company of the women in the village. Since she came to England she hardly ever went out. There were no women with whom she could sit and talk, laugh and joke, plot and plan. The outside world she saw on her television screen was hostile and lonely. Occasionally she would smile at her loneliness, remembering how she had believed, and her friends would still believe, that life here was free and comfortable and without problems.

The raid this morning had frightened her. She had not understood at the time what the police wanted. After they left, she felt that somehow they were just like those arrogant policemen who used to terrorize the people of her village. She had been more frightened of these, however, for at least in Pakistan she knew where she stood with them and what they said. The reality of what she saw in England had shattered the illusions with which she had grown up.

She looked across at her daughter who had fallen asleep on the sofa. At least life would be different for her. She would go to school, learn to read and write. She would perhaps grow up to be like those white girls, not listening to parents, wearing obscene skirts and going round with many boys. Jalib's mother liked and hated white women. She hated them for the power she felt they had over her – English was their language, this was their culture, one which had no meaning to her, locked as she was behind the walls of her own house, like a prisoner. She liked them, for at least they could laugh and joke. All laughter had been erased from her life since she set foot in this country. She was left with an empty feeling and loneliness, always longing to be back in the company of her friends who came to her now like ghosts from some far-off dreamland.

She started to think what Jalib would be doing. She had no idea of the sort of life he lived once he left home. Out there, the world was totally alien to her. Because she felt so estranged from her son, she missed the company of her women friends even more. She had once complained to her husband that she did not like the sort of life she was living and that she felt ever so alone. She had told him that she would like to go back to Pakistan for a short while. He had become angry and had shouted at her for being ungrateful. 'You have nothing to do all day! Why can't you be content?' Fearing her husband, she had never again raised the issue. She had wanted to tell him that there was no joy left in her life, that she felt imprisoned in her own home, that she hardly knew the people who lived across the street. But the days when the two of them would sit and talk to each other had long since gone.

Whenever her husband shouted at her, she would sink into herself and remember how gentle he had been in Pakistan. Even after a hard day's work in the fields, they had loved and joked with each other. On the days when they had had an argument, never for one moment would he be violent with her. In all those years, he had never hit her. He would talk to her for hours, promising that some day they would come to England and make

59

a good life for themselves and their children. But from the day she came to join him, he had been distant from her and the children. He came home at 7.45 every morning, ate and went to sleep. He woke in the evening, ate and went to work. In Pakistan they had talked about the harvest, about how much money they owed, about the state of their livestock, and so many other things in their lives. Now she no longer knew what it was he did. She knew he worked in a mill, but had never seen one and could not say anything about it. They were estranged, cut off from each other by walls of incomprehension.

As Jalib was usually out for most of the night, she worried that perhaps he would become like the white boys and forget his parents now they were getting older. She had never, in her dream of dreams, imagined that the youth of her son would waste away before her eyes. She had seen her uncle leave the village and go to Karachi searching for employment, only to come back a broken man. It hurt her profoundly to see her son wasting his life, but she felt sick in her powerlessness to help him. What had happened to her uncle – could that ever happen to her son?

Apart from the walls of her house, her children, and the fear of her husband, there was now no other life for her. Only on Saturdays would she go into the town centre and do her weekly shopping. Now and then she would ask Jalib to take her to visit relatives or sometimes they would visit her. Even the birth of a son, still celebrated with the distribution of *ladoos*, failed to bring her people together. The sweets were usually brought round to the house by someone. There were no gatherings of women with whom she could chat and laugh. All that was now a memory, buried deep in the life she had spent in her village. Now she called out for the company of her women friends in the loneliness of her dreams.

She stood up, sighed, and switched off the television. She carried her daughter gently to the bedroom. Then, downstairs to the cellar to make everything ready for her husband, when he returned in the morning.

'I suppose that loafer will be hungry when he comes back,' she said to herself as she made some chapattis for Jalib. Watching the *roti* roast on the *tawa*, her thoughts travelled to somewhere called Birmingham, to Maqsood.

Chapter 8

'Oi!' Hussain got off a bus and shouted to them. 'Where you lads going?'

'Here comes the worker,' Jalib said jokingly to Mohan.

'Where you lads going?' Hussain asked again.

'Nowhere, man. Just killing time. Been sitting in the library all day. Me bloody arse has got blisters,' Mohan replied.

In fact, he and Jalib had been talking about Hussain just before they left the library. Hussain was one of the few lads they knew who actually had a job. He worked in a mill, like Mohan's and Jalib's fathers. 'Shit job, I hear,' Jalib had remarked. Even so he was jealous. Having any sort of job would make his own life a million times more bearable. 'He won't keep it long,' Mohan had said. 'He can't keep his gob shut. You watch, he'll be shit-stirring. He'll get the sack. What's this capitalism and stuff he keeps going on about?' Jalib had shrugged.

'No luck with a job yet?' Hussain asked, with concern in his voice.

'Oh yeah! We start tomorrow. How about buying us a tea over there?' Jalib pointed to a café across the road.

'Man, all this bumming around gets me down. Café after café. Nothing ever happens around here!' Mohan protested.

They were now in the café. Talking and laughing. Hussain was telling them the details of his job at the mill. The number of workers, the number of hours he put in, the amount of money he came out with. 'They're bloody racists,' Hussain continued. 'The union is pathetic. You talk to the shop steward and he thinks you're his personal coolie. Conditions are bad, man.'

'For God's sake, let's talk about something else for a change!' Mohan was getting very irritated with Hussain because he couldn't imagine the situation. He had never worked.

'Sorry, lads. It's just that I can't talk to anyone there. The lads are shit-scared. Whenever I say anything, they call me a commie and atheist, and all that sort of thing.'

'Yeah,' Jalib replied, 'we're cowards. That's what it is. The bastards come to our homes and take our people away and we don't do anything about it.' His voice spelled out his pain and anguish, anger and frustration.

'No, Jalib. We're not cowards. The whites tell us that and we believe them. Look at our people back home. Thousands died fighting the British.' Hussain frowned, sad to see Jalib's despondency. 'Look what our lads did in Southall a few weeks back.'

Jalib had been filled with a sense of pride at the youth explosion on the streets of Southall following the murder of Gurdip Singh Chaggar. When news of the murder had been announced, he had sat in shocked silence, a sense of impotence overwhelming him. But hearing about the rebellion of the youth of Southall, Jalib and Mohan and a few friends had joined in a celebration. They had gone round the streets of Bradford, as though trying to capture the freedom and power they saw on the television screens. Stealthily they had written on the walls, LONG LIVE SOUTHALL and SOUTHALL FIGHTS. Every time they went past these grafitti they felt the wall captured a few moments in their lives which held some true meaning.

'I don't see nothing happening here,' said Jalib. 'We just don't care enough about each other. We just sit and take whatever gets thrown at us.'

Hussain looked sympathetic. 'I hear the pigs came to your house, Jalib. Some lads were talking about it at work. Did they get Maqsood?'

'No!'

'Don't worry about it, brother. That's not going to get you anywhere. We got to fight them.'

'Fight? How, man?' Jalib asked desperately. Perhaps Hussain could show him a way to help Maqsood, a way round the frustration he felt at his father's acceptance of everything as inevitable.

'You should come to our meetings,' Hussain answered. 'We can discuss ways of fighting.'

'Can't come to no meetings, brother. Too many things on my head. Ain't no commie, either,' Jalib replied.

'We get shit from all the *goras* all the time. What are those long-haired louts going to teach us, man? I been to one of your meetings,' Mohan continued. 'They tell us how bad life is. I *know*, man! I don't have to be told. Besides, they look down on us as though we're some kind of shit. Them sort of meetings ain't no good for us, brother.' Mohan looked away towards some of his friends who had just come in.

'What I mean,' Hussain pressed on, 'is there is no short cut in the struggle against imperialism. Meetings can be a drag but we have to learn to talk things over.'

'Look, brother, I don't mean bad, but they no good to us. You keep it up and we're with you at the end. But none of these commies is going to look down on me. No, sir!' Mohan said confidently, recollecting the meetings he had attended and walked out of, bored or, where his interest was caught, in disgust.

'You can't treat all white people the same. After all, there aren't that many of us in this country.' Hussain felt unable to give a clear answer. He too felt the pressure of the patronizing attitude to blacks at the meetings. He had tried to explain this to his comrades but they laughed it off. He had been given a job of organizing amongst the Asian community. Always he confronted the same distrust and suspicion in his friends – that these *goras* and their revolution were beside the point. He felt the much-heard rhetoric spring to his lips: that blacks were a small minority and therefore had to stop talking about separatism. But if he stopped to think, he realized that only the white members talked about separatism . . . Hussain's need to feel he was doing, achieving something drove him on, pushing aside his scepticism. He wanted his two friends on his side. They looked by turns impatient and bored as Hussain continued to talk, justifying and defending his membership of the International Socialists. He explained to Jalib and Mohan that the most important thing was to build the revolutionary party and that other things were secondary.

'Me and us folk being stuck on the dole, that don't matter?' Mohan demanded. He felt disgust rising in him. 'My cousin phoned from Southall last night. Wicked, man. The bastards cut "NF" into this lad's arm and chest.' Mohan made a motion as though cutting 'NF' into his own arm. 'I suppose that's nowt to get worked up about?'

'Of course it matters, brother. You're on the dole because capitalism's in a crisis.' Hussain tried, in vain, to explain his organization's line of thought. 'Fascists thrive in a period like

63

this. That's why we call for black and white unity.' Hussain felt clearly that his reply was like a drop of water in the angry waves of a hostile sea. In his heart he felt more unity with Mohan's fury than he felt with the central committee of the new party that the International Socialists were creating. He caught Jalib's eye and for a moment Hussain thought they understood each other.

Hussain had been brought to Britain as the son of his uncle. At the age of ten he had been dragged from the arms of his weeping mother. Whenever he thought about his life back in Pakistan, it came to him in vague images, like a fading dream. He recalled the love and tenderness with which his mother had brought him up. Memories of her lived deep inside him, but even so they were clouded by the poverty they had shared.

His had been the poorest family in the *biradari*. By coming to this country as the son of his uncle, Hussain became a treasure-chest incarnate to his family. He had only to grow up and go to work. The money he would send home would raise his father and mother, for the first time in their whole lives, out of the clutches of the money-lender. When he boarded the plane that brought him to Britain he was aware, child though he was, that the misery of his family was supposed to fly away with him.

His early days away from his mother had been painful, but with the passing of time he forgot his need of her. His letters home became less frequent. His mind became enmeshed with the fast-moving sophistication of life and school in England. His letters home stopped altogether.

Coming home from school, his uncle would tell him over and over again how fortunate he was to be in Britain. Hussain would be overcome with shame that he was having to live off his uncle. There was not enough gratitude in him, it seemed, for him to thank his uncle properly. Although he was a schoolboy, he felt deeply obliged to repay his uncle, at least with money.

Without Hussain knowing anything about it, his uncle wrote to his mother the moment Hussain was old enough to leave school. He complained in the letter that Hussain was a burden and he should leave school and start work. Hussain's mother wrote back, advising her son to do just that. For the first time in his life, Hussain raised his voice against his uncle, furious that his mother should be used in such a way. This only served to increase the terrible sense of guilt he felt when in his uncle's presence.

Sitting down to eat with his uncle and aunt, guilt and resentment stuck in his throat. He hated them for never having bought him a single toy or shown any kind of affection for him in all the years he'd lived with them. But what did this matter, he had to ask himself, compared to the debt he owed them for bringing him to Britain in the first place? Instead of taunting them with his resentment, he suggested that he should leave their house.

'It's your life. I'm not going to stop you,' his uncle had coldly replied. He finished his food and got ready for work. 'There is nothing more I can do for you,' he said.

Although Hussain had been sincere when he raised the subject, deep down he felt that his uncle should swear at him and tell him not to be so stupid. The knowledge that his uncle really did want him out of the house hit him like a ton of bricks. The world outside was suddenly a terrifying place.

'Your auntie will give you ten pounds,' his uncle said. He then calmly left the house.

In a flash, Hussain's world flew into confusion. A comforting thought came rolling out of his turmoil, the truth had now come out. With this thought he felt a little easier. He walked into his bedroom, not really feeling anything, and packed whatever clothes he could into a little old suitcase. He took the money from his auntie. Without saying a word he walked out into the evening. He noticed that his auntie deliberately avoided his eyes. It was apparent from the way she acted that she had discussed this matter with her husband and was in total agreement with him. Hussain concluded that she too was happy that a burden was being got rid of.

Hussain had been nearly sixteen at the time he left. He met an English school-friend and stayed with his family for a while. When he explained his predicament to some of his teachers at school, he was advised that he should leave and pursue his studies at college.

The first few months of living away from home had been extremely rough. He had more often than not gone without food. But it wasn't long before he learnt to survive without money or a place to live. He slept in one house or another. Until he met up with a group of latter-day hippies, he merely roamed from friend's house to friend's house. With the hippies he found a sense of senseless security. With them he drifted in the bizarre life of hallucinogenic reality.

His generally curious nature and his youthful sense of rebellion led him on a number of occasions to fall foul of the law. On more occasions than he could remember, he became involved in ugly battles with gangs of drunken white youths who wished to conclude their Friday night's boozing with a spate of 'Paki-bashing'.

Hussain was not to know, in fact the thought had never crossed his mind, that his mother had been left torn, bleeding and confused when her only son had been snatched from her. The pangs of separation had been made worse when Hussain ceased to write to her and she felt as if she had never had a son. When Hussain did learn of the pitiful state his mother had been reduced to through his insensitivity, he sat and wept for many hours. He wanted to go back to Pakistan immediately but he was trapped in a financial crisis. Whenever he had any money he sent it home to his mother. His letters home became much more regular. But he just could not save enough money both to send some home and go back to Pakistan himself.

He often envied Jalib and his other friends when they talked about their families, for he could not really understand what an orderly family life and home meant.

'My father thinks you're a fishy lad,' Jalib said to Hussain. 'He thinks that if I hang around with you I'm going to get myself on the wrong road.'

Hussain was hurt but he knew parents were often a bit apprehensive when they found out their sons were associating with him. People who go on demonstrations and such would not be liked by the police.

'Does your father think you're a bloody angel, then?' Hussain sarcastically replied.

On Sundays, Hussain usually stood in front of cinemas or other places of cultural activity to sell his party's literature. He was well-known to many people and through the arguments that took place when people approached him he fully understood the way people viewed him. But he continued his activities unperturbed, always finding a rhetorical slogan to justify himself.

Chapter 9

She had finished reading the Koran for the morning. She carefully, and delicately, wrapped the cover round it, kissed it, humbly touching her forehead to it, took the *Siparas* from the children and placed them high on the shelf.

'Get on. Get ready for school,' she told the children who, without much ado, went to their room and started filling satchels and putting on their uniforms. It was over a month since she had watched, with apprehension, the raid on the house opposite. She had talked about it once or twice with her mother but generally the subject was quickly buried. Although she knew they had come for Maqsood, she did not like to mention his name as it always filled her with fear.

Six months ago her mother had told her that she had found a fiancé for her. Her mother's nephew. He too was called Maqsood. Each time his name was mentioned, Shaheen's body froze with terror. Her parents recognized her apprehension, but assumed it was because of her bashfulness, and that all girls behaved like this. Shaheen saw this stranger as a potential master. Ever since they broke the news to her, she had sat for many hours in her bedroom, crying, always trying to hide her tears from her parents.

She had tried to explain to her mother that she did not want to get married as she was too young, and she did not know what he would be like. Her mother had tried to comfort her by saying that her parents knew what was best for her. Besides, she said, it would help her sister's impoverished household, having a son in Britain and working.

Shaheen had talked about her dilemma to her friends, who had given her much sympathy and comfort, but almost all of them were caught in much the same situation. They had all told her to do what they dared not do: 'Tell your parents you will not marry him.' Each time she would look at the face of the girl giving the advice and would see in her eyes that this was not the answer.

There was no way she could simply say this, as her parents would automatically assume she was having an affair with someone else, that she had become like the *gorian* who had no respect for their parents. As a way of delaying her marriage, she had convinced her parents that she should be allowed to go to college and further her education. After much reluctance, they had agreed. Shaheen knew that this pretence of further education would soon come to an end.

She stood looking out of the bedroom window, watching for a sign of her father and brother coming from work. She heard the noise of an approaching car, an opening and shutting of car doors. As soon as the children heard the front door open, they ran down the stairs, screaming and shouting with excitement. Shaheen picked up her *dupatta*, covered her head, and descended.

After serving breakfast and clearing up, she made a last inspection of the children as they prepared to catch the school bus. It was 7.45 and they were among the hundreds of local Asian children who were 'bussed' away from the area to other schools because of the policy of the local council. On many days, she had collected the children as they returned from school, dazed by sleep and weariness from the journey. She would curse the authorities for making them suffer so much stress. She has written many letters to the headmaster and to the education authorities about the 'bussing', but nothing had come of them. The children, now ready, ran out of the house. The bus was waiting at the end of the street. They boarded it, waved back at her, and disappeared for the day.

Walking to college, she saw the shopkeepers laying out their displays. Fruit. *Dahl*. Other goods. In their windows, posters advertised the latest films to arrive from India and Pakistan. All around her, cars and buses went to and fro. Students rushed to their lectures, rubbing the night's sleep from their eyes. Her *dupatta* now dangled half off her head. She felt the interrogating gaze of many unseen eyes as she walked along. She jumped as a car beeped its horn and swerved towards her.

'*Ohai sohaniay!*' a man shouted from the car window, blowing kisses at her.

'*Harami!*' She cursed as she picked up the books she had dropped with fright. She looked up at the ugly face of the man who had shouted to her, as the car sped down the road. Cursing him, she pulled herself together. The heads of passers-by had turned in her direction. One of the women who was entering the shop nearest her said, '*Ghoonday*, daughter! They forget they have sisters and mothers of their own!' Shaheen nodded in agreement, grateful for the support this woman gave her, and then walked on.

As she went into the college, she folded her *dupatta* neatly and entered the lavatories. She released her hair from the *parandha* which bound it to the back of her head, put some make-up on her face and re-emerged feeling a different person.

'So your dad doesn't mind you looking for a job?' Shaheen asked Kiran.

'He does and he doesn't. Since he's been on the dole for so long, it's hard to make ends meet at home. So he says if I can find a respectable job it's alright.' Kiran's father had been made redundant over a year ago. Now that the redundancy money was all gone, it was impossible to run the house on his unemployment benefit and maintain his family obligations back in Pakistan. 'I've got an interview next week,' Kiran continued smiling, 'wait and see what happens if I get it.'

'What is it?'

'It's in a mill.' They burst out laughing. 'I don't see why I can't do it. After all, he's worked in a mill all these years and me brother works in one as well.'

'But they won't look at it like that. It took all my courage just to come here to college.'

They had talked of these things so many times before, always trying to find new solutions. They were sitting in the common room, another haven for the unemployed and idle of the town. By coming here, they felt a sense of security, a sense that they were furthering their lives, when, in reality, they sat here all day in the company of other unemployed young people.

'I've been hearing you have an admirer, Shaheen,' Kiran said, looking across at Jalib, who had entered the common room and was trying to hide himself behind a group of people congregated around a pinball machine. 'Talks about you all the time, you know.' Shaheen was looking intently across at her admirer.

'He's a bloody child!' Shaheen replied, 'Thinks I don't know; he's always hanging around our house. One of these days my Dad's going to catch him and make him into a real Ranjha!' She laughed with Kiran, and then became engrossed in their conversation.

'It's so unfair,' Shaheen continued, 'I don't want to marry him. I haven't been back to Pakistan since I came here.' She recollected what she could of Pakistan. She had left when she was eight. The only memories she had were of playing in the fields with other children from her village. She often tried to imagine what life was like in Pakistan but could find no parallel with her present existence. She asked her parents on a few occasions to send her back for a holiday but they had always replied that they could not afford it.

'I've said no so many times but Mum thinks that it's 'cause I'm shy,' Shaheen continued. 'Like hell I'm shy! I just don't want to get married!'

'You can't tell them anything,' Kiran replied, 'they seem to think that that's all there is in life. Get married and make lots and lots of babies. I told my father that I'll get married when I want to. He used to be really hard on me when he was working. Now he just sits around and doesn't say much. I think it's because I'm trying to get a job that he doesn't say anything. I suppose if I get a job he couldn't marry me off, could he?'

'My Mum and Dad just won't listen. I suppose I'll just have to be strong. I hate the weekends. You just can't get out of the house. There's always someone coming round. That bloody kitchen drives me nuts.' Shaheen had to hide herself in her bedroom if men came around, and cook endless meals, make tea and wash up.

Kiran had stopped listening: she shunned thoughts of her home. She was looking at Jalib with mischief in her eyes.

'Oi, Jalib!' Kiran shouted across the backs of the congregation lounging around the pinball machine. 'Come here a minute.'

'Stupid cow! What you done this for?' Shaheen whispered to her. Jalib looked around and, noticing the voice came from where Shaheen was sitting, he turned back, pretending he had not heard.

'Looks like the big man's a bit shy,' Kiran said, slyly.

'Leave him alone. Don't call him over here,' Shaheen told Kiran emphatically.

'Would you like a cup of tea?' a young man asked Shaheen. Shaheen and Kiran looked at each other, then at the young man

70

and thought that he was a pathetic little creature. 'Tea, indeed,' thought Shaheen.

'Piss off,' Kiran answered him. Immediately he disappeared into the crowd. They laughed. Kiran felt mischievous again and looked across at Jalib.

'Jalib!' she yelled, grinning all over her face.

This time Jalib could not pretend he hadn't heard. He was too near. He turned round, filled with embarrassment, and slowly walked towards them, thinking that everyone's eyes were focused on him. It was common gossip that he had a soft spot for Shaheen. Jalib looked around, hoping that Mohan was still hanging about and would go with him. He sat ill at ease, next to Kiran.

'Give us a cig, will you,' Kiran asked. Jalib nervously pulled out his packet and handed it to her. 'What's wrong? Have you seen a ghost?' she asked him.

'No. What do you want?'

'We were a bit bored and thought you might come and cheer us up,' Kiran replied.

'I suppose you're trying to tap a cup of tea. I'm skint. Honestly,' he said.

'Say, is your Maqsood alright?' Shaheen asked. She flinched at the name.

Kiran had gone to the counter. Jalib felt very uneasy. He wondered whether Shaheen too felt this strange uneasiness but she looked perfectly calm to him. 'Is that what you wanted to talk about?' he asked, gaining some confidence. He was trying to assure himself that Shaheen couldn't possibly know how he felt.

'No.'

Jalib felt confused. 'Perhaps she does feel something for me,' he thought.

'I didn't call you,' she said coldly, cursing Kiran for asking him to come over. He looked like a scared mouse. She felt like laughing at him but refrained, as she did not want to embarrass him further.

Kiran returned with the tea. 'That's all I can afford. The rest's the bus fare home.' She handed Jalib a cup. 'Me and Shaheen will share.' Shaheen nodded agreement.

'I hear you got an interview next week, Kiran.' He paused, then continued, 'Hope you get it.'

'Get's round fast, don't it? I don't know, I hope so,' Kiran replied. 'It's a bit rough at home.'

'Have you had any luck?' Shaheen asked Jalib, who felt easier now but still sat stiffly. 'You don't have to behave as though we're strangers – after all, we live opposite each other.'

'I'm not nervous!' Jalib butted in.

'She never said you were!' Kiran teased.

Finally Jalib managed to free himself from them and rejoined his friends. Shaheen stood up and looked across at him. The common room was almost empty. In a few minutes the security men would come round to clear everyone out. The present occupants would then flock to some other place of congregation for the unemployed.

'I'd better go. It's getting late. I'll see you tomorrow.' Shaheen went straight into the lavatory. She tied her hair neatly into her *parandha*, unfolded her *dupatta* and removed her make-up. As she was walking out of the main doors of the college, she turned round and noticed Jalib coming towards her. She held the door open, but he turned and walked back.

'Bloody coward!' She cursed him and walked out towards her bus stop. Although it was still light she never walked home as the fear of being attacked always loomed menacingly over her. It was a fear which hung over the head of every woman. Only recently a young student had been brutally murdered in the labyrinth of streets leading to the university and the college. Shaheen thought of the murdered woman, cringing as she stood near the people waiting at the bus stop.

Sitting in the bottom deck of the bus, she watched the familiar scenery of Bradford pass. She handed the conductor her fare, her thoughts now moving from the momentary freedom she felt when she was with her friends to the anxiety of her home. She seldom thought about her college work because she understood the farce that it was in her life. She understood that it was nothing but a device by which she could get out of her home. But at the end of this term she would finally be locked up behind the walls of her home, only occasionally venturing out to help with the shopping.

Even in the relative safety of the common room she was nervous as she sat and talked with boys, in case someone should inform her parents. But she longed to join in the discussions the boys had. Someone would start a conversation about the attacks on black people that were happening up and down the country,

72

or about how bad the unemployment was and that something should be done about it. Although she had tried many times to participate in these discussions, the boys had told her to shut up. She felt anger at them for not understanding that she too cared, and she also felt bitter at her own position, knowing that she could go no further than having a conversation about these things. Her parents would never consent to her participating in any activities that might bring the family name into disrepute. The closest she ever came to participating in anything was when she saw a scene on television or read about the events in the newspapers. She would imagine herself running amok in the streets, letting herself loose on the forces that bound her to this life. She was torn between the never-ending struggle of her family's existence and her own struggle against the coming marriage.

Only in the loneliness of her own room did she ever contemplate her sexual life. It was as though sex, as understood by her white friends, existed only on television or in fiction.

She reached home and quietly opened the front door so as not to disturb her father and brother who were sleeping. Throwing her books on the settee, she greeted her mother. 'Mummy, I'm back!' She said this in a gentle voice as she popped her head round the kitchen door.

'Have you forgotten you are a Muslim,' shouted her mother from the cellar, 'or have you become a *goree*?'

'*Aslam-O-Alaikum,*' she corrected herself. 'What brought this on?' she asked her mother, as she walked down the stairs.

'You should always greet people with *slam*,' her mother said as she roasted the chapattis on the *tawa*. Shaheen felt uncomfortable in the heat and smoke of the cellar. Her mother looked harassed by the amount of food she had to cook. She was a bit behind schedule.

'I'll just go and change, Mummy,' Shaheen said.

Her mother threw another chapatti on the *tawa*. 'Set out the plates and then go and wake your father and brother,' she said.

Shaheen walked up the stairs. She threw her *dupatta* on to the bed, quickly changed, picked up an old *dupatta*, put it over her head and then went to knock on her father's door. After waking up her brother, she went down the stairs and started to lay out the plates.

'Go and see if the children are coming up the street,' her mother said, coming out of the kitchen, 'it's nearly six o'clock.'

Just then there was a knock on the door. Shaheen opened it and the children ran past her. Her father was coughing and rubbing the sleep from his eyes. He lovingly pushed his way past his children who were clinging to his legs as though they had not seen him for a long time. Shaheen looked at the children's faces. They looked tired from the long day's travelling and schooling.

The meal finished, the men went to work. The children went to their bedrooms to do their homework before they went to bed.

'What do you do at college?' her mother inquired.

'Just go to classes and things,' Shaheen replied.

'Oh.' Her mother sat back in silence. Although unhappy that her daughter was out of her sight for such long periods, she prided herself on the thought that at least her daughter could read and write, whereas she had never had that opportunity. Most of the time, when she was not busy with household chores, she would sit and think about her daughter's wedding. How she would arrange everything! Of course it would be nothing like weddings in Pakistan but at least she would be able to forget herself for the duration of the ceremonies and be able to give her daughter all the things she had been saving for her wedding over the years.

'We got a letter from your auntie in Pakistan this morning,' her mother said. Shaheen shuddered, for she knew that the letter would be about her marriage. 'She's very anxious to get the marriage over with as soon as possible.'

'I've told you before, mother. I don't want to get married. Not yet anyway. I want to continue with the college,' Shaheen replied. She crushed her anger as she did not want to insult her mother.

'You are a grown woman now, Shaheen. People say all sorts of things behind your back. When I was your age, your brother was running around.' Her mother paused and started thinking that perhaps her daughter had fallen into bad ways, then refused to pursue these thoughts further.

'Mother, there is so much I want to do,' Shaheen protested, 'I haven't even seen Maqsood.'

'I suppose you want to find your own *khassum*!' her mother said angrily. She could not understand her daughter's attitude.

After all, she thought, what was good enough for her was good enough for her daughter. 'What do you think you are? A *goree*?'

'No, mother.' Shaheen spoke through the tears which were beginning to gather in her eyes. 'It's different now. Here, I mean. Back in Pakistan, everyone knows everyone else. By the time the marriage takes place, you've grown up together.' Shaheen refrained from using Maqsood's name again. If she did, she could never use it without insulting it, she thought. If that happened, then God help her.

'We're not forcing you. I know he's a nice young man. Good looking. You'll have a happy life. It will help your auntie ever so much. She's so poor.' On seeing Shaheen's tears now rolling down her face, her mother's attitude softened. But she persisted, telling Shaheen that she knew what was best. Her mother thought back to the time when she too had refused, and how her family had slowly broken her resolve.

'I know what I want in life, mother. It's not to cook and be like a slave to someone I haven't even seen! Please don't do this to me.' Shaheen wiped the tears from her eyes.

'No one's saying you have to get married tomorrow,' her mother tried to comfort her. 'Besides, you have to think about the family honour. Stop crying like a little girl! You'll have plenty of time for tears later,' her mother said sarcastically. She thought about the number of weddings she had helped organize. Each time, as the *doli* left, the bride had cried. She too had wept when her *doli* had left her parents' home. Such a long time ago.

'You are forcing me. Everyone's forcing me!' Shaheen looked at her mother. She wanted to ask whether her youth had been forgotten. She wanted to ask whether she really cared about her or whether it was for the *biradari*. But she stopped herself, for she loved her mother dearly and did not want to hurt her feelings. She stood up and left the room.

Her mother sat in silence, wondering where she had gone wrong. She had tried, she thought. She had brought up Shaheen to the best of her ability in the ways of Islam. When she had asked her eldest son to marry, he too had refused point-blank. She had not pushed him, for he could do nothing to dishonour the family. No one ever gossiped about the sons. It was the daughters who held the burden of *izzat* in the family. She sat silently, trying to understand where she had gone wrong. Maqsood was set on coming in the next few months. She had hidden this from Shaheen, for she feared that if her daughter's attitude did not change then the family's name would be damaged forever. Her position would be ruined forever in the *biradari* and in the community.

Chapter 10

The dark and satanic mills, about which children sing in hymns at morning school assemblies, could be seen in every direction. Tall, ugly chimneys sending endless messages to the heavens. Ageing mills, whose profitability had depended on the introduction of cheap labour. Now many of the 'cheap' workers sat around idly killing the hours on the dole. Those still working spent their lives in tense anticipation of the day when their redundancy would be announced. Every morning, sleet or snow, rain or storm, at the corner of every major building in every part of town, workers in ones and twos waited for their transport to work, each with his bundle of food dangling from his wrist in a leather bag.

Hussain stood under the shelter of a loose billboard which advertised an Indian film. The cinema was redundant now. The introduction of video had all but shut down the Asian cinemas. Hussain blew into his hands to get some warmth from his breath.

Through the miserable morning rain he could see the faces of workers coming off the night shift, the rain rinsing the hard work from their eyes. Looking at them Hussain thought that here, in a land where they were supposed to find prosperity, they had found only sophisticated oppression and open and crude exploitation. Almost all the workers he saw in the mornings and on his way home in the evenings were employed in similar run-down mills. From the bodies of mill workers returning from work a smell of yarn always radiated. In the faces of older workers Hussain always noticed a look of placid acceptance of this reality. A look of lost youth; a defeated generation. Whenever he argued with the older workers the same theme was always put forward. 'It is as Allah would have it. We have come here to work. Work, son. Make money and go back. You young people have had life easy.' Many old hands had said this to him.

'Always on time,' he thought, as he saw his lift approaching. 'I hope I don't let these lads down one day by sleeping in.'

'*Slam*, brother,' he said in greeting, shutting the miserable coldness of the morning out as he climbed into the car. As Hussain and his work-mates entered the gates of the mill, the workers from the night shift were leaving. They waved to each other, yawning. Walking past the now-stationary machinery, Hussain wondered how many workers had stood in front of these monsters.

After changing into his working clothes, Hussain looked at the clock. 'Ten minutes to go yet! Too bloody early again.'

'How are you, Badshahow?' Hussain shouted to one of the older workers who had already started working. He had worked there, in the winding section, for as long as anyone could remember and always started fifteen minutes earlier and finished ten minutes later than anyone else. 'As God would have it,' answered the worker, frantically trying to keep up with the pace of the machine.

Hussain looked at him, eyes filled with anger and sorrow: sorrow at the sight of this pathetic man who was enslaved by a winding machine, afraid of losing his job. Hussain knew that this fear was one of the reasons the older workers were bound mercilessly to the whims of the machines. The older workers knew if they lost their jobs, for whatever reason, they would not find other employment. But Hussain felt anger as well. He thought this very process, where older workers frantically attempted to maintain their fast-fading usefulness, was itself a shackle for them. Few of the older workers would entertain any notion of becoming involved in a union or any notion of unity with other workers, despite the long tradition of brave struggle they had behind them.

As the clock's hands approached 8 a.m., machines roared into life from various corners of the department. The overlooker, from his office, looked across the floor and then buried his head in his morning newspaper.

In the spinning department, Hussain was in charge of either two or three sides, depending on the type of material being used. Each side had 144 spindles on which yarn was spun. Older white workers said that when the second-hand machinery was brought in some years ago, one worker was employed on each side. Now the spinner had to move from side to side, ensuring that none of the 432 threads broke. When a thread did break, a smooth join had to be made.

'It's wrong, though,' Hussain said while eating his lunch. The Asian workers sat together round two tables eating their lunches. The white workers sat in twos and threes, eating their sandwiches. 'By law, we are entitled to two breaks, apart from lunchtime.'

'You get them, don't you?' replied the older worker from the winding section, hastily filling his mouth with a piece of chapatti. 'You get out here in the morning and then again in the evening. That's a break, isn't it? Or do you just like complaining?'

The Asian workers started at eight o'clock in the morning and finished at eight o'clock in the evening. The white workers started at eight and finished at five-thirty. The management allowed only one official break, forty-five minutes for lunch. Fifteen minutes each was allowed in the morning and again in the evening, providing another worker tended the machine while the operator went for a rest.

'But we don't really, because when one of us goes for a rest another one has to do twice as much work. So the break is not a break at all because all the machines keep running,' Hussain continued, looking across the mouths of fellow-workers, being hurriedly stuffed with food. 'You don't even take a break. I mean, the winders are allowed to stop their machines, but you don't. You work like an ox. What for? Bonus? It's a fiddle. Because you work so hard the other winders get into trouble for not producing as much as you.' Hussain was almost shouting at the older worker. The white workers were looking across at the Asian workers, to see what the excitement was about, then they continued eating their sandwiches. The older worker looked deeply into Hussain's eyes, attempting to see how much anger was there. But he had heard all this so many times before, he was used to it.

'You do your job, son. It's not your fault. You're still young.' The older worker sighed.

After eating, Hussain washed his hands. He looked at the now stationary machines. The silence soothed his ears. He pulled out a chair for himself and sat looking through the loading area into the yard below.

'No point talking to him, brother,' said one of the workers from the twisting department, who had come to sit with him. 'We've all told him but he won't listen.'

'How long has he been here?'

'Don't really know. He's the oldest one of us. I think this was the first job he took when he came from Pakistan.'

The older worker had worked in the mill for so long that he was viewed as part of the machinery. It was a joke among the other workers that if his lift was more than a minute late he would take a taxi to work, thus losing more money on the taxi fare than he would earn in a day's work. For all his punctuality and hard work, he had started here as a winder and after all these years he still worked as a winder, on the same machine. Younger white workers had been promoted to higher positions but, like everything else in his life, he never questioned this. Life for him revolved in and around the mill.

'Once the union man came,' the twister continued. 'He asked if we wanted to join. All of us thought it was a good idea. I think most of the *goras* joined too, but I'm not sure. Once there was some trouble between the winders and the supervisor. They stopped working.'

'Did the others stop as well?' asked Hussain.

'No. Anyway, the manager came and said they should start their machines and then he would listen. You know, most of us couldn't speak English. The union man came. He said we should start the machines and he would talk to the manager. All the winders refused to start except for the old man. He said it wasn't important. When he started his machine, the union man said we should all be good boys like the old man and start our machines. He said it was best to talk things over.' The twister flicked his cigarette into the yard. 'Anyway, every one of them started working. Since then no one's really bothered about us lot on the day shift.'

Hussain sat in silence, thinking, filled with anger and frustration, both at the union official and the old man. The textile unions were notorious for their racism and open connivance with management. Asian workers always viewed union officials with contempt, comparing them to corrupt government officials back home.

'There is a lad on the night shift. He's always going on about unions. There's still supposed to be a union here, you know. Only we don't know who's who. The union man never comes nowadays. And the shop stewards are all *goras*.' The twister stopped talking. He looked at his watch to see how long this blissful rest would continue. Hussain listened intently while the twister told him various stories about what had happened over the years. He looked at the twister, as a pupil looks to a teacher. He found the wealth of experience buried in each of his fellow-workers, their endurance in the face of endless obstacles, the contradictions in the life of the older workers who, through the fear of poverty and their obligations to their families and loved ones back home, had had to succumb to such harsh justice, all this was eloquent far beyond the sterility of the meetings he had attended. All the rhetoric that was churned out at meetings by various speakers meant less and less to Hussain.

The twister told him of the night-shift worker who had on many occasions attacked the union official for not listening to grievances. Their discussion was interrupted by the noise of the workers in the canteen packing sandwich boxes, moving chairs, occasionally laughing, indicating that lunchtime was almost over.

'Right, lads,' shouted the overlooker. Hussain cursed him under his breath. He had been deeply engrossed in the twister's tales of the struggles that had taken place in the mill. Hussain was deeply touched by the tone of the twister's voice, indicating the resentment he felt deep down because he could not speak English. Whenever there was a union meeting, a rare enough event, it was always conducted in English. This automatically excluded the involvement of Asian workers who, although they could understand only occasional words, still attended the meetings.

Hussain noticed the older worker was already working, as he walked back to his machine. He shook his head. Although he thought it was workers like that old man who stopped or destroyed any unity, he would not allow himself to hate the man. He realized the old man's acceptance of these conditions was still part of his heritage. As Hussain watched him running frantically in front of the machine, it seemed to him that the old man's soul had been dragged from his body by the winding machine. The sight also frightened Hussain. Could he end up like that? Just another piece of ailing machinery, frantically trying to keep pace with an ailing monster.

From different directions the machines came to life. The overlooker scanned the shop floor, his face showing the comfortable feeling that all was running smoothly. After one quick glance, he buried himself in a crossword in his paper. Hussain's body bent awkwardly as he joined a broken thread and thought about his conversation with the twister.

'Must meet this guy,' Hussain thought, referring to the night-shift worker the twister had told him about. Ahead, he saw the task of organizing the work-force. Then he looked at the old man. 'Not going to be easy with people like him around. Wonder if he'll spill everything to the overlooker?'

When in company with other workers, particularly the old man, Hussain talked with reserve, fearing someone might report him to management. He had resolved that the more obstacles he saw to organizing the work-force, the harder he would work. He moved mechanically from one broken thread to another, time slowly crawling towards the evening.

Chapter 11

After the first few 'coincidental' meetings at bus stops, Jalib had stopped his act of hiding his feelings for Shaheen. He began to meet her in various parks around the city. At all these meetings, he tried to avoid directly mentioning what he felt for her. Shaheen had spent hours telling him what life was like for her at home, her dreams of employment, of anything that could free her from her impending doom. Lately, she had come to feel very relaxed in Jalib's company.

As arranged, they met at midday so that they could spend the rest of the day together, walking through the park. Deep inside the park, they sat down. They were both fearful that someone would see them. Jalib talked briefly of events that had taken place since he last saw her. Shaheen sat, uninterested, fidgeting with a broken twig. Sensing something was wrong, Jalib stopped talking and looked away towards the pond. There was an island in the middle of it. The dirty grey water, which always smelled stale, was rippled by a flock of ducks swimming towards the island. The background was serene. Tall, lean trees. Small hills covered with thick bushes. Beyond this, in the middle of the park, an old museum stood, like a relic from a bygone era. In the trees, above their heads, birds landed and flew away. In the far distance, the sound of the city.

'Jalib.' Shaheen spoke with a slow and quiet voice, her head bowed towards the earth. She dug the twig into the earth. Jalib sat with his back towards her, his head bowed, his body filling with fear at the unknown tone of her voice. For a moment they sat in silence. Awkwardly Jalib turned round, his eyes watching Shaheen's hand as it dug the twig into the ground.

'We talk about all sorts of things, Jalib, but never about what matters most.' Her voice said more than her words. In all the time they had spent together, they had always avoided discussing their feelings for each other.

'I know.' Words that he couldn't control were beginning to

form on his lips. 'I've been trying to . . .' he stopped. The next line would not come out.

Shaheen was perplexed by her feelings. Feelings she had never felt nor expressed in the company of any man before came to her in tidal waves, riding on the fears of her family, her life, her engagement to Maqsood in Pakistan. They sat in silence, their silence expressing a melody more deeply than spoken words ever could. The silence of the park and the stillness of its greenery were in total contrast to the turmoil inside each of them. The ducks, the only creatures near by, had reached the sanctuary of the island.

Shaheen looked up from the earth she had been digging and saw Jalib's bowed head, sharing her thoughts, feelings and fears. She placed her hand gently under his chin and lifted his head. Jalib watched her hair blowing softly across her shoulders. They looked deeply at each other. Shaheen moved her hand across his brow, feeling the warmth which embarrassed and burnt her body. Jalib felt her hand cut gently through to his brain. They fell back on the grass, joined as a single being. What words could not say, their bodies sang, half naked now, a tune of joyful bliss, hidden from the eyes of any onlookers by the thick bushes.

Combing the tell-tale blades of grass from her hair, she looked about her to make sure that no one was near.

'Why do you look so down, Jalib?' Shaheen said, brushing the sleeves of her *kameez* and shaking her head to push back the hair which flowed carelessly around her face. 'It's not that bad, you know.' She spoke confidently, although she felt some dire calamity had descended on her, shame and fear that someone should find out what had happened.

'It's just that I didn't want it to happen like this.' He spoke with a tone of sadness in his voice. He sensed Shaheen's fears but pushed them out of his head, his mind preoccupied with dreams of a Heer–Ranjha * type of romance.

'Things don't happen the way they do in those films, you know,' Shaheen said, asserting herself. She felt let down. He was behaving like a lost child. Jalib saw before him scenes from Indian love films, Shaheen singing and dancing among beds of roses.

'Will it end now?' Jalib half-whispered in a cracked voice. He
* Famous Punjabi lovers.

felt as though, because of what had happened, he could no longer see his love develop to a film conclusion.

'You're ever so silly!' Shaheen smiled. 'Why do you feel like this? We still have each other.' As she finished her sentence, the ghost of Maqsood came hauntingly from Pakistan and landed in her head. She felt a sadness engulf her. In all the moments of her life, with the passing of each day, she felt the time approaching when she would have to submit herself to a man she was beginning to loathe. She grabbed hold of Jalib's hand and held it. Tightly, as though by doing so she could dispossess herself of the ghost. The warmth of Shaheen's hand cleared Jalib's thoughts. Their long eyelashes saluted each other's gaze. Jalib bent towards her and tried to embrace her in a passionate kiss.

'Stop it now, stupid! I've got to go home.' She lovingly pushed back his face. 'One bit of grass in my hair and you can say goodbye to your dreams, lad.' She pointed to the ducks. 'Look! See how carefree they are!' Her *dupatta* waved in the breeze behind her; her hair was now neatly wrapped in her long *parandha*. Reaching the gate, they stole a last glance at each other, then walked in opposite directions, both concerned lest someone should see them coming out of the park together.

Jalib found Mohan sitting on a patch of grass outside the Job Centre. Mohan was reading a newspaper someone had left behind. The headlines announced another woman had been murdered in West Yorkshire. 'Some Bengali guy got murdered in Brick Lane, I hear,' Mohan said. 'Funny how it don't get into the papers?'

'Shit. It's bad down there, init?' Jalib replied. He had heard of the murder from a friend who had recently come from London. Although it frightened him, he saw this as a London phenomenon, not one that had relevance to his own town.

'All that's coming here, though,' Mohan said, as though Jalib had spoken his thoughts aloud. He paused for a while, thinking apprehensively of his relatives in Southall. 'Any day now someone here is going to get murdered.'

Jalib nodded in agreement, then stretched in the grass, looking at the slow and graceful movement of clouds in the clear blue sky.

'Isn't that Dalair Singh?' Mohan pointed to an old man slowly dragging his bulky frame towards them. Jalib lifted his head and looked in the direction that Mohan pointed, nodded agreement and closed his eyes.

Dalair Singh moved slowly along the pavement. Old age had robbed his eyes of almost all sight. He slowly and deliberately moved to the point where Jalib and Mohan sat, unaware that eyes were focused on him, his white hair shining like a flag of silver in the sunlight. All around him he felt the society he had fought, moving, throbbing, buzzing with life. A long, grey coat, down to his knees, flapped gently in the breeze. Every now and then he would stop, caught in a fit of coughing. He'd spit phlegm into the road, slowly wipe his mouth, and return his handkerchief, neatly folded, to his pocket.

Dalair Singh was a veteran freedom fighter from the days of the British Raj. He had lived through the turmoils of the Indian uprising, through the Second World War. Old age and relentless work in the mills of Bradford had broken the physical strength of his body, now passing into its final stages before resting in eternal peace. Even with his body a mere shell, awaiting the inevitable embrace of death, his spirit of rebellion and his will to resist surpassed that of the young. The murder, suffering and hunger that he had seen during the heyday of the Raj had instilled in him a sense of resolve to struggle. He often recounted stories of guerrilla raids against the occupying forces of British colonialism. Now his legs were plagued by rheumatism, but he still went to any demonstration to which he was invited and with which he agreed.

As Dalair Singh approached, Mohan shouted to him to come and join them. He cautiously changed direction and slumped down next to them. Jalib sat up, as a sign of respect in the company of an elder.

'Well, sons, still haven't got a job?' Dalair Singh asked a general question.

'There's no jobs anywhere, *baba ji*. Don't bother looking any more,' Jalib replied despondently.

When he talked to Dalair Singh, he never felt uneasy as he did in the company of other elders. They often talked about Dalair Singh with the respect they would give any other elder, yet they never thought of him as any other elder or as some venerable old man. He was not like other old men who made sure that everyone knew their age and their wisdom and who, on that basis, expected respect.

86

'You must agree: never give up. That's what they want you to do – give up.' Dalair Singh stopped to cough and clear his throat. 'You are young. When I was your age hardly anyone worked for money. Oh, there was their army. We saw what that was.' He again paused. Whenever he talked to a youth, his aching body would fill with excitement as he relived the days of his past struggle. Jalib and Mohan were completely mesmerized by his presence. They saw in him a strength which they felt they did not possess. Dalair Singh continued talking about how India had not really changed much, as far as the people were concerned, since the days of the Raj.

'True, the English aren't there any more, but the people are still oppressed and hungry. The Indian ruling classes are thieves and bandits – like all ruling classes. We've no real independence.' He stopped. 'I get out of breath nowadays. You must come to my house some day and listen to some songs that I recorded a long time ago. Not those filmy ones, but about life and struggle.'

The police station dwarfed everyone, rising dark and menacing in the background. A small trickle of people came and went into the Job Centre. All three of them sat with their backs turned to it. Dalair Singh now talked about the Indian film industry and the songs it churned out.

'Why do they make these films?' he continued, with immense passion. 'All they tell us about is a dream that has no meaning in the lives of most of the people.'

'But that's what our lot want,' Mohan protested, 'We've got to move with the times. Films are supposed to make you forget yourself and live somewhere else for a bit.'

Dalair Singh spoke after a pause, choosing his words carefully. He did not want to seem to be defending the old ways. 'When you hear those songs with those *gitaran* and things – do you like that sort of music?' Jalib and Mohan nodded in agreement. Dalair Singh continued, 'These songs are meaningless, like the songs on television. Why, in a village back home there are more instruments than in an English orchestra. We're a rich people culturally. When they make these songs like the white folk, they sing the tunes of imperialism.' He paused again, thinking that perhaps he was beginning to alienate these youths. 'You should come to my home some day and I'll play you music that sings about our people's struggle.'

'We will come,' Mohan said, feeling a bit uncomfortable.

'Ah. I see you are restless. Perhaps you think this old man doesn't know what he's talking about.'

'No, no, *ji*,' Jalib half shouted, on realizing that Dalair Singh had been hurt by their insensitivity. 'It's just that here we are bored all day. I mean, why should we care about what went on so long ago?'

'Every new weapon is useless until one learns to use it. For us, we must make our history into a weapon. We must learn from each defeat.' Dalair Singh spoke with wisdom, seeing before his eyes the scenes of the massacre of the gardens of Amritsar. Soldiers with their rifles targeted at the congregation of people, only one exit, a gap of about four feet. Frantic running and screaming amidst the cracks of gunshots. General O'Dwyer, commending his soldiers for not missing a shot, dying in a pool of his own blood. Rich Indians, upper-class ladies, in their fur coats, gentlemen in their neatly pressed dinner suits, all diving behind chairs for cover from the bullets of the pistol of Ubham Singh. Ubham Singh signing his name in symbolic unity of the peoples of the subcontinent, 'Ram Mohamed Singh'. Dalair Singh sighed as he saw the image of Shaheed Ubham Singh dangling from the hangman's rope, and came back to his youthful audience.

Feeling that perhaps he had bored them, he gently rose. Mohan helped him and shook his hand firmly, clasping it in both of his. Dalair Singh carefully walked down the small slope of grass, cars like vague blurs passing before his eyes. All around him, the mother of the monster he had lived to fight. Soon he dragged his ageing frame out of sight of Jalib and Mohan.

Some friends of their own age stopped beside them on their way to the Job Centre.

'Our kid here, Mister Luck himself. Man!' one of their friends said with tears of laughter rolling down his face, his arm around the shoulders of his friend about whom the story was being told. 'Went to McCann Alloys – looking for a job, the fool. On the gate there was notices in Urdu, Punjabi, Gujarati and Bengali,' he stopped to catch his breath, 'SORRY NO VACANCIES.' They all rolled hysterically on the grass, wrapped within the frenzy of the laughter at their predicament. 'What's more, our kid can't read any of them!' The laughter went louder still. The passers-by turned their heads, out of curiosity, and continued with their lives.

Chapter 12

'How many of them were there?' Hussain asked Mohan, who sat in front of him twitching nervously.

'Four,' Mohan answered. Anger and excitement poured from his mouth as he recounted the story of how his brother had been attacked that morning. It was early Sunday, and Malkit had gone out to play with his white friends in Shipley, a small town on the outskirts of Bradford. As they ran around in the park, a group of four skinheads walked up to them. After swearing abuse, they started to kick and punch Malkit. They told his white friends that they should not mix with wogs, as they are dirty. Frightened, the white children had run away.

As Mohan was telling the story, Jalib and a few of his friends walked into Hussain's flat. Hussain had also phoned some of his other friends and asked them to come.

'Were they ordinary skinheads?' Hussain inquired, his voice cool and calm.

'There's no such shit as ordinary skin, man! They all wear the uniform of Paki-bashers!' Jalib butted in, infuriated that Hussain could be so cool when Malkit had been beaten up.

'What's he like now?' Hussain asked, turning to Mohan.

'Not bad. Just bruises and things like that,' Mohan muttered.

By now, Hussain's flat was occupied by around twenty youths. In their faces it could be observed that their concern was not only for Malkit. Over the past two years the town had witnessed an increase in racist abuse and acts of violence. On some working-class estates, which were surrounded by Asian families, not one of them dared to live. If a black person walked through there in the hours of darkness, it was not unusual for some missile to be thrown in his direction from a hidden vantage point.

It was the same all over the country. Everywhere, areas of black population were caught in the grips of organized attacks by racist thugs. 'Paki-bashing' – a phenomenon which had begun to subside in the early seventies – had re-emerged, embodied menacingly in gangs of working-class white youths. Skinheads, who had at first been rebels against authority, were now being given special status by various fascist organizations. In some areas, particularly in the East End of London, skinheads were being recruited by Nazis. The time when racist obscenities were written, under cover of darkness, in lonely passages of flyovers and subways, had now passed, to be replaced by their logical enactment – attacks on black people.

Now the room in Hussain's flat buzzed with excitement. A poster of Soweto hung defiantly on the wall. In it was a picture of a young man, tears in his eyes, carrying in his arms a boy who had just been shot. In the background, someone carried a placard saying, 'Don't mourn. Organize!' The eyes of some of the youths would stop at the poster, then sink into deep thoughts about their own situation.

'They always get away with this, brother,' said a youth over the heads of the others who were arguing with Hussain. 'Thing is, it's not just our Malkit who's been done over. It could have been any of us who had been there – me or you – I mean, we can't let these bastards get away with these things all the time.'

'What I'm saying,' Hussain replied with a look of apprehension in his eyes, suggesting perhaps he was not saying the right thing, his voice sounding indecisive, 'is that not all skinheads are the same. We can't just go around beating up any old skinhead. We need support from working-class white people. Black and white have to unite.'

'Skins aren't ordinary people, man!' the youth shouted back. 'I ain't going to walk with no shit, man! They want to come with us, then let them burn their gear. These guys are killers!'

'I don't know about you guys,' said Mohan, who had been sitting silently and listening to the discussion, 'but I'm going to kill one of those bastards. It's my brother they hurt! Those bastards have to be taught a lesson! You guys can talk all you want, but I'm not going to give them just a "scare" . . .'

Again the atmosphere in the room changed, this time to one of vengeance. A solid mass of feeling hung invisibly, like a curtain.

'He's our brother, too,' Hussain said, realizing the mood had changed to one demanding immediate, retaliatory action. 'It won't make much difference if we just go out and sort out a few skins,' he insisted. 'What we've got to do is to be in a position where we can mobilize the whole of our community.'

'I say we go to Shipley,' said Jalib excitedly. 'We take *dandas* and things with us. Skins hang around Nab Wood Park. If they're there, we'll clobber them. If not, then we let them know that we came and that we mean business. And maybe we'll find the ones who did this. Does your kid know who they were?' Jalib stopped to ask Mohan, who explained that one of them was called Tim, and that he knew the street Tim lived in, but not the house number.

The smoke-filled room contained an air of frustration as the small gathering, shut away from the lives of people of their community, articulated a movement of the community. Outside Hussain's flat was a cavalcade of cars, but no one took much notice of what was happening. This part of town was usually full of Asian youth on Sundays. Today was warm and sunny, there were many people on the streets. All smiling and generally merry. It seemed as though the unusual summer's sun was itself burning away people's problems. Judging by the way they moved up and down these streets, one would think they were satisfied with their lot. Underneath the smiles and jollity, and the clean, smart clothes, however, was a hidden torment. A sense of insecurity, of fear and also a longing for its expression. But there was no channel for the people's voice. In stark contrast to the sounds of passing cars, the colourful clothes on the street, inside Hussain's flat everyone was serious. The gathering agreed that they should respond to the attack on Malkit, but not in such a manner that it could have adverse effects on someone else.

'Right then,' Hussain brought the discussion to a close. 'We know what we're doing. I think what brother Jalib said is right. We've got to be in a position where we can counter such attacks against our people. For today, we'll basically have a show of strength. If it does come to confrontation, then we're well prepared.'

Mohan had finally been won over to a position where he would see it, not in terms of a personal vendetta, but as part of a wider process. Reluctantly, he had agreed that, for today, they should have a show of strength and that they should all get together again to see if they could form an organization.

Some of the youths had already gone in their cars to obtain weapons, while those who remained moved around in Hussain's flat, talking and laughing with excitement. Hussain opened the windows and the room slowly started to clear of the smoke.

Jalib stood in the corner of the room, staring intently at the poster of Soweto. He felt a sudden sorrow at the tears of the young man carrying the corpse of a loved one. His eyes travelled to a different poster. Although he had known Hussain for many years, these posters told him about Hussain's life, which he knew in part, but about which he understood very little. Looking back to the poster of Soweto, he felt that the poster, with just the picture, expressed so much, whereas inside himself he could not find the words he wanted to describe what he felt. Hussain had gone into the kitchen to make tea for the youths waiting for the cars to return. He came back and placed a large tray on the table with cups of tea on it.

'Help yourselves, lads.' He indicated the cups of tea. 'You're going to need it!'

Hussain's words were greeted with an awkward laugh. During the discussion, Hussain had become acutely aware that, for all the time and energy he had spent working with the International Socialists, and then the Socialist Workers' Party, he had achieved nothing. It had been Jalib who had articulated most of what was decided about being in a position to mobilize the whole of the community. Whereas he, Hussain, for all his involvement, was stuck with slogans – 'Black and White – Unite and Fight'. Hussain looked across to Jalib and felt that in him there was something he did not have himself. Whenever Hussain talked to people, he always talked about politics and about struggles that were taking place in various parts of the world. He felt that Jalib, unlike himself, did not gloss over the reality of black people's lives with empty phrases. He was aware that his relationship with the youths who had come to his flat was different from that with his earlier associates, because it was based purely on incidents. Conscious that this relationship lacked many things, he went over to Jalib, in whom he saw the rebellion of youth and the humility of his people.

'Tell me, Jalib, why don't you like the slogan, "Black and White – Unite and Fight"?' he asked in a very humble manner.

'I'm a simple bloke, you know,' said Jalib sincerely. 'I didn't say I don't like it. It's just that I feel that we've got to get our own house in order first.' Hussain listened intently as Jalib continued,

'I mean, look at us, man. We're not together at all. And you and your lot go on about "Black and White – Unite and Fight". Yeah. We have to fight together with the whites. But we'd better sort out the muck in our own gardens.'

Hussain hummed in agreement. Although he was tempted to repeat his much-used argument on this subject, he felt that what Jalib was saying was correct.

'You know, I came to your meetings once or twice,' Jalib went on. 'I don't trust those guys, man. They don't really care about us. They are always going on about this racism stuff. One thing I don't understand is why they don't sell their stuff in the areas where these racists live. I mean, we're not the racists, are we! Yet they always come pestering us.' As Jalib talked, he gained the confidence that he had lacked while the discussion was going on about the skinhead attack. It was clear to Jalib that Hussain's organization just wanted members and that they were not interested in the plight of black people.

The car horns sounded outside. This was the signal for everyone to leave. 'Let's go, lads!' A voice broke to a sudden euphoria of excitement. There was a quick movement of youths. Some grabbed coats and ran down the stairs and out through the door, shouting. The cars were parked on either side of the road. Heads turned in the direction of Hussain's house, curious at the twenty or so youths gathered outside. Malkit sat in the front seat of the first car.

'Let's have a look at you,' Jalib said to Malkit, leaning over the window while the others got into the remaining cars. 'Didn't you hit them back?' he joked, relieved that the bruises were only slight.

'They were big boys!' Malkit's eyes expressed puzzlement at the sight of so many people. He was clearly proud that the bullies were going to be taught a lesson and that they would know how it felt to be at the receiving end of an attack. He also felt proud of Mohan for having so many friends. Beyond this, he was still a bit dazed from the attack.

'Don't you worry now – we'll get them,' Jalib patted Malkit on the head and then sat in the car behind.

Now full of warriors, the cars moved slowly into a cavalcade. Jalib looked behind him and a feeling of power came over him at the sight of the mighty army following. In each car, youths were singing loudly to Asian music, as though singing the last song of warriors going into battle. As they drove along the busy roads, pedestrians and motorists alike looked in bewilderment as they sped past.

'I suppose they think we're going to a wedding,' Hussain said to Mohan who was nervously twitching beside him. 'Yeah, brother, we're going to a wedding alright,' the other occupants replied in unison, laughing nervously.

'Skinhead land.' A youth in the first car broke the silence which had overtaken them all, the same silence, like a blanket of apprehension, which had descended on all the cars.

'Where to, brother?' the driver of the first car asked Hussain.

'Straight along the road and we'll come to Nab Wood Park.' A faint nervousness could be detected in his voice. It was difficult to tell whether this was due to fear or excitement. As the cars came to stand along the edge of the park, a group of middle-aged white women looked across at them and then pretended they had not seen them. Hussain, Malkit and Mohan got out of their car. The others remained inside.

'Whereabouts do they hang out, Malkit?' Hussain asked softly.

'Over there. They meet in a shed,' Malkit answered, pointing through some bushes which blocked his view.

A gentle breeze blew in Hussain's face as he looked across in the direction Malkit pointed. He stopped and thought, and then went from car to car telling the occupants to remain inside for a while.

Nab Wood Park is well known. It sits at the bottom of tall and proud-looking hills. A small group of shops loosely and awkwardly greets the observer's eye, across the park, beneath the dense woods on the hills. Going around the side of the park is a small road, which has the appearance of a canal surrounding a castle. The greenery of the park, the heat of the sun, the clear blue sky, were far from the reality of the lives of the youths who sat impatiently in their cars.

Hussain, Malkit and Mohan moved slowly deeper into the park. The others, as arranged, alighted from their cars and moved towards the shed from different directions, making sure they were not seen by its occupants.

The suspense with which they entered the park was broken on learning that none of the skinheads was there today. A group of white children were playing football near by. The shed was a small building – a shelter for the people who came to the park. Inside it was crawling with grafitti – 'Wogs out', 'Death to the Blacks', 'NF', 'BM', and an assortment of other insults to black people, barely legible. This was one of the places where unemployed white youths, who had been won by racist propaganda, congregated. Their hatred of black people was shown on every wall of this shed. The grafitti spoke ominously of the future for black people. It told of the anger and frustration of *lumpen* white youth who had swung to racism.

Hussain shouted to the white children, one of whom walked towards him and said, 'Is there going to be a scrap, mister?' He had assumed that these people had come here to have a gang fight with the skinheads. 'Don't beat us up, mister, we're not skinheads.'

'No one's going to beat you up, lad. Do you know where they've gone?'

'Don't know. They could be anywhere.'

'You tell them that we came looking for them,' Hussain continued, 'and we know where Tim lives. If any of our lot gets roughed up again, we'll come knocking on his door.'

'Okay.' Then the white boy ran off, occasionally looking back, and busied himself in his game of football.

Fifteen minutes later, they were lying on the grass and generally idling under the sun. Jalib shouted so that everyone could hear, 'No point hanging around here. The bastards won't come back today.' There was reluctant agreement.

'Thanks for coming, lads,' Mohan shouted. 'Well, we did come for a show of strength but it's a pity there's no one here to show it to!' A laugh raced across the park.

Slowly the youths made their way back to their cars; the white women who had seen them enter and pretended they hadn't were still there, standing with their baskets of shopping, and talking as though oblivious of the presence of these youths who were a a long way from where they lived. As they drove back homewards, they went past a police van parked just at the end of the road coming into the park. It had obviously been there a long time.

'Shit, man,' Jalib commented, seeing the van. 'How long the pigs been here? Look sharp, lads.'

Chapter 13

Whenever Dalair Singh talked to Hussain or any of his friends, he was always conscious that there was no other way for them to learn the real history of their nations except through the memories of old men such as himself. But Dalair Singh was different from the other elders of the community, who disliked many of his ways and indeed often criticized him. Elder Sikhs did not like him as he did not believe in Sikhism. Furthermore, he would endlessly argue that Sikhism was never meant to be a religion but a way of life, a philosophy. Whenever he made references to Guru Nanak,* it was with the utmost respect, but he maintained that Guru Nanak was essentially a poet.

Dalair Singh particularly enjoyed Hussain's company and the many questions he would ask. He told Hussain of his own childhood, tilling and working the land in the burning heat of the sun to help feed his impoverished family. At the end of the year's toil, he would sit with his family, filled with terror, waiting for the Raj's tax man to come and take the *sarkari* quota away from them. Already, although so young, seeing his year's work stolen from his family, Dalair loathed the tax man.

His father had told him, 'Our hunger will not go away until the English leave. They'll never leave unless we make them. Only then will we eat our *roti* in peace.' His tired old hands removed his turban and his long hair caught the wind.

From that day onwards, Dalair Singh had gone wherever he heard whispers of protest. Then, in 1931, the whole of the Punjab was shaken by the news that some of its sons, led by a young man named Pagat Singh, had bombed the Assembly Hall. Pagat Singh was hanged, shouting slogans of freedom that opened Dalair Singh's eyes to the world-wide context of his people's struggle.

Hussain asked him why it was that amongst all the men who had come to fame as martyrs of the struggle for independence in India, there was hardly any mention of Muslims.

* Nanak (1469–1538) founded the Sikh religion.

'Even you, most of the time, talk about Sikh martyrs, *baba ji*,' Hussain commented. 'Why is there no mention of Muslims?'

This question made Dalair Singh criticize himself and the way he talked to people about his recollections of India. He understood that not much truth was written in history books, for, more often than not, the historians of India were English-educated Hindus.

'Perhaps I talk about Sikh heroes because I identify with them,' he answered Hussain thoughtfully. 'But Habib Noor should be given a place in our history alongside Pagat Singh.'

Hussain listened intently as Dalair Singh told the Muslim hero's story. Habib Noor had fought against the occupying forces of the British in and around Peshawar. A colonel of the Raj had opened fire on innocent people in the Kisa Khani Bazaar. Habib Noor had avenged their deaths by taking the life of the officer who had ordered the shootings. He had been caught virtually there and then.

'They tried him the same day, and condemned him the same day,' Dalair Singh continued. 'They put him in a limestone furnace and poured boiling water on him until he died.'

Hussain listened with anger and frustration at his own ignorance. Whenever Dalair Singh talked of the year 1947, Hussain's mind would fill with the images from the old man's memory, headless corpses littering the roadside, vultures eating their fill, blood-stained walls. Dalair Singh's eyes would flood with tears. The monumental movement of population that followed the creation of Pakistan had shocked him, as had the murders, the looting and rape.

'The massacres didn't happen as they tell you in their history books,' he told Hussain. 'The English history books lie. The British, as they were leaving, paid huge amounts of money to organize young Hindu thugs under the Jana Sang, who went, with the full blessing of the British, to bring hell down upon the Muslims. This was the way they fostered the riots. A monsoon of blood came, my son.'

Hussain would try and envisage the hell Dalair Singh and others must have gone through during the year of partition. Dalair Singh explained that many had gone to prison while the independence movement had been gaining strength in India. Those who later took up the leadership of India found that their days behind bars had turned into a mountain of wealth. Of those that history does not remember, Dalair Singh would say, 'They are like a young widow who gives birth to her dead husband's child and the child also is dead. She must spend an eternity in mourning.'

Hussain would be filled with shame and sorrow when he saw Dalair Singh weep. He had not seen many old men crying. Only when Dalair Singh talked of his son did Hussain feel that he could identify with the old man's world. Dalair Singh had been in England when his son was arrested in India, following a strike of railway workers in Madya Pardes. Dalair Singh had written to his son in prison, telling him not to be sorrowful, but to keep up his struggle on behalf of his impoverished fellow-workers.

At the mill, Hussain had recently met Ghulam B. Azad, the night-shift worker about whom he had heard so much. Azad had recently been elected shop steward and he was much more active at the mill. The regional organizer of the Dyers and Bleachers Union had made many visits to the mill on learning that the union was becoming more active. Once, when the workers had held a meeting to discuss their demand for higher wages, Hussain had been surprised to see that even the white workers attended. Ghulam B. Azad was the only Asian in the whole work-force who was a shop steward. He spoke vociferously about demanding another 20 per cent rise. He called for an indefinite strike if management refused. Although he spoke well, he could not talk English fluently.

When the demand was put to management, it was refused, as everyone had expected. Management said that the workers were being ridiculous and that the company could not afford such a pay rise. In fact, management refused point-blank to negotiate on the demand, so the work-force decided to strike as soon as they heard. From the first mass meeting, a delegation had been elected to go and put their demands to management again.

Hussain had accompanied the delegation and a heated debate had developed between them. It transpired that the regional organizer for the union had got wind of the threatened strike and had talked to management about a possible settlement, seeking grounds for a compromise. Before the delegation went into the meeting, the regional organizer and the general manager had met separately in one of the offices.

'What do you mean, you already had a meeting with management?' Azad shouted at the organizer. His words were not coming across clearly in English, but the tone of his voice was easily understood.

'That's my job, brother. I'm your regional organizer.' The word 'brother' nearly made Hussain vomit. Ghulam B. Azad had told him to be very quiet and not say anything as he was new and was likely to be fired if management suspected he was politically involved in anything, or could articulate his views in English. Hussain felt a burning desire to hit the regional organizer, but restrained himself, as advised by Azad. He listened impatiently as the regional organizer continued in a cool, calm manner. It was evident from his discussion that he had been involved in many disputes like this.

'I have had a long chat with Mr Leach, the general manager. He is a very reasonable man. He showed me the books and I can assure you lads there is no way that the company can pay 20 per cent.' He paused for a while to let the delegation understand his words. The delegation contained only two Asians, and only one of them was a proper delegate.

A long, heated argument followed between Ghulam B. Azad and the regional organizer. Azad accused him of going behind their backs. He called him a liar and said that the company had been making millions of pounds' profit over the years and that the regional organizer was deceiving the workers by what he said. While this was going on, he managed to whisper to Hussain in Punjabi that it was strange that none of the white workers had said anything. Although Hussain didn't have a clue what he was talking about, he nodded in agreement.

'The management have agreed to a very reasonable offer of 5 per cent,' the regional organizer continued, looking at neither Ghulam B. Azad nor Hussain. Instead he looked at the white workers, all of whom were in supervisory jobs, and all of whom agreed with the regional organizer.

'That's no fucking good!' Azad shouted, infuriated by the manner of the regional organizer. 'I have a wife and kids – what's it going to do for us?'

100

His weak command of English did not deter him from expressing his feelings. The regional organizer sat and listened calmly to his cursing and shouting, as though this was quite natural and part and parcel of his job. Each time Ghulam B. Azad swore at him, the regional organizer would glance over at the white workers, as though saying, Look at him. Can't be grateful that we allowed him in. Wants more money. These wogs are getting out of hand nowadays.

Eventually it became obvious that argument was getting them nowhere. The delegation stood up to go and face management. All walked in. The office was neatly laid out with plants and paintings. A picture of the Queen hung just above the manager's head.

The regional organizer went up to the manager and shook his hand, as though they were old business partners.

The manager sat down again while the regional organizer explained that negotiations had reached a deadlock. Although no names were mentioned, the manager looked at Ghulam B. Azad with cold eyes.

'Well, gentlemen, I take it that Mr Crawley has told you what my position is in this matter.' Without looking directly at any of the men standing in front of him, the manager continued, 'At present I have nothing further to say. Thank you, gentlemen, could you go back to work now. All this is costing us a lot of money.' Azad and Hussain reluctantly followed the white workers out of the door.

When he came back outside, the regional organizer went to great lengths to talk to the rest of the work-force. He explained what he had been able to achieve for them and that they had no choice but to accept.

'If you lads continue with this silly action of yours, Mr Leach told me – and he's an honest and good man – that he will just close the mill and sack everyone. You know what it's like for jobs, lads. Especially for you coloured lads. No one is going to take you on anywhere. You should be grateful to Mr Leach for not laying you off.' He continued in this fashion for over twenty minutes. Azad had shouted that they should not listen to him and that he was a traitor to them. The regional organizer, it appeared, had enlisted the support of the old winder from the day shift. Together, they managed to put so much fear into the

Asians that they would be sacked and that no one wanted black workers any more, that the men had slowly gone back to their machines. The night-shift workers, who had come in for the meeting, went home to catch up with some sleep.

As the regional organizer was leaving, he seemed to be full of the joy and satisfaction of a job well done. He did not look at Ghulam B. Azad as he made his way back to the manager's office. When he disappeared from sight, Azad turned to Hussain, who was about to start his machine. 'I bet he was going to get some bribes for what he's been able to achieve. Dirty dog!' Azad swallowed his anger at this open treachery. As he got ready to leave, he continued, 'I tell you, the *goras* got a special deal. I've been here for many years and I know how they behave. I mean, I can tell you the reason they looked contented was that they got what they wanted. Anyway, they're not workers. It's all a 420, just so that the union remains in their hands.'

'A 420?' queried Hussain, ashamed of his ignorance.

'It's the section of the penal code back home relating to fraud, son,' Gulam explained patiently.

Hussain listened to what Azad was saying and understood now his earlier comments. It was also more than likely that the management had used the age-old tool of 'divide and rule', Hussain thought.

'After you've been here a few months, then start getting involved more in the union.' These were Azad's last words and farewell for the day.

All around Hussain machines roared to life and were going endlessly through their monotonous motions. Hussain was running frantically around his machines, trying to join broken ends. Every time the machines started after they had been shut down for a while, almost every other thread would break. Riding above the roaring of the machines was a feeling of a lost battle from the work-force.

Hussain, angry and infuriated, tried to concentrate on his job and pushed the thoughts of what had happened out of his head. For once in his life, he felt that he had to move with caution and not let his rhetoric get the better of him. 'Capitalist bastards!' He cursed the manager and the regional organizer as he bent to fix a broken thread.

When he looked up, he noticed that his bobbins were almost

102

empty on one side and felt he had no strength left to put them all up. There were 144 bobbins on each side, each one weighing about twenty pounds. At the same time as he put them up, he had to ensure that they didn't stop or that not too many threads broke at any one time. Hussain gave a sigh of relief as one of the workers came to his assistance.

'Don't get too depressed. You'll get the hang of it in time.'
'Thanks, brother,' was all Hussain had the strength to answer.

Chapter 14

Two weeks had passed since the skinheads' attack on Malkit. It had now faded into the background. The feeling that it had stirred up on that day now lingered loosely in the conversation of the participants. With the fading sense of urgency, all discussion about the need to organize had dissolved into oblivion, except that the event had left a deep mark on Jalib, who, on numerous occasions, had talked to his friends, suggesting they should get together. Beyond this, matters did not move.

Two days after the incident, Shaheen had come to learn of it through Jalib, who mentioned it in such a manner as to leave her thinking this was basically a man's job. She felt hurt by his attitude, as though she did not exist for him apart from the times when she was with him.

Over the past few weeks, she had come to feel very lonely when she was not with Jalib. With the passing of each day, she would become more depressed as she saw the ghost of her fiancé coming a day nearer to materialization. She tried to find in Jalib a refuge from her approaching marriage. Her parents no longer questioned her as to whether she consented to the marriage. They took it for granted that she would not refuse. Shaheen knew that her outward signs of depression were still interpreted by her parents as bashfulness. She saw her life and her plans slipping from her. To add further to her pains, she had developed a deep love for Jalib. On occasion she had said, in jest, that they should run away together and get married. Although she had laughed at this, deep down she knew that it meant more to her than just a passing joke.

On the days she had arranged to see Jalib, she would wait nervously for the hour to arrive and then, on the pretext of going to a girl friend's house, or something similar, she would leave home, always shutting the door behind her, in fear of being discovered. She would move quickly to the appointed place, her head full of the depression of her approaching marriage. Walking along, she would shut herself off from the world that threatened her and let her thoughts turn to love and bring into her being the warmth she felt in the company of Jalib.

Today, as she walked to meet Jalib at Hussain's flat, she could not remember how long it had been since she last saw him. One week, two weeks, she could not remember. Over the past few days her mother had been frantically running around, making preparations for her wedding. Although she lived opposite Jalib, it was rare for them to meet. If they did meet each other, they acted as though they were strangers. When she saw him accidentally, her heart would jump with a longing to put her arms around him and caress him. If ever their eyes met in the street, she would be filled with happiness, with the knowledge that he loved her dearly. Understanding their positions, both would smile deeply inside themselves and then turn their backs on each other quickly, continuing whatever they were doing.

As Jalib opened the door, she hurriedly ran in, her heart full of fear in case someone should see her coming to the house. As soon as she entered, she asked Jalib whether anyone had seen her. He comforted her, saying that he had been watching the street and there were no Pakistanis around. Hearing this, Shaheen relaxed and flung herself into his arms.

'Where's he gone?' she asked, referring to Hussain.

'Oh, I managed to get rid of him for a few hours!'

Although she was filled with joy at being able to see Jalib, still her heart was sickened with worry and grief. She had spent the whole night thinking about her relationship with Jalib, and of her marriage. After many hours, she had buried her head in her pillow and wept. She had tried to wash away her problems with her tears and had somehow fallen asleep. On waking, all her life's misery came flooding back. Today she set her mind on clearing up some of her life. She didn't know what or how she should do it, but felt that she could find some way out of it, if she seriously put her mind to it, all the time knowing full well that all the possible avenues were closed. Still, she felt that she could not just give in like this.

'Stop it, for God's sake, Jalib!' She spoke as she freed herself from his lustful embrace. 'Can't you see that I'm all worked up and sick with worry?'

'Don't you love me any more?' His manner seemed extremely

sluggish and unconcerned about her and her feelings. This hurt her deeply.

'Of course I do, stupid.' She put her hand through his hair with affection. 'There's more to life than loving each other. Think about poor little Shaheen for a while instead of feeling horny all the time!'

This comment made Jalib feel guilty as he had almost forgotten her marriage was so near. The prospect of her marriage suddenly filled him with a deep remorse. They were now both well aware of what their lives had in store for them. An invisible but tangible shadow of depression descended on the room and for a short time they sat in silence. At this moment they were one, both understanding the reality of their relationship.

Shaheen felt a mass of confusing and painful emotions stir in her. Although she knew that her love was reaching a point where she would have to part with it, she sat enjoying the company of her lover and trying to take as much comfort as this moment would allow. She wondered whether Jalib really thought of her predicament with as much caring as he suggested, or whether it was just a ploy to get into bed with her. Tears began to roll down her cheeks as she thought about the sudden change which would soon come.

Looking at Jalib, through a curtain of tears, she noticed that he too was crying. She felt engulfed in sorrow and hugged him tightly. A whirlpool of confusion, pain and anguish clutched her in its merciless grip. Venus rode the waves only in mythical dreams of dead Greeks. Now there were no gods of love driving past in chariots of fire. Here was her family, struggling to keep afloat on tides of crisis. Back in Pakistan, her relatives struggled to fight off their poverty. In the midst of all this, she was caught.

'You're supposed to comfort me!' she said, as she pushed back her tears. 'Not cry with me. It's not you who's going to have to get married.'

'Sorry, Shaheen,' Jalib replied, not really knowing what he was saying. 'Shall we still love each other, do you think?'

'We can't just stop loving each other, silly.' She felt a sharp pang inside her when Jalib spoke these words. Like a child, she thought, not even understanding what's going on. She felt a maternal love for him.

Shaheen thought about her parents. She hated them for making her go through this hell. But at the same time she loved them for the tenderness, affection and care they had given her. By insisting that she marry Maqsood, they thought they were doing the best for her. They were protecting their own way of life, which was threatened from all sides. It hurt her intensely to see her father slaving night and day to pay for her wedding.

She and Jalib talked about this for a long time and they both agreed that they did indeed truly love their parents. They agreed it was completely wrong to show their parents disrespect or swear at them as white kids swore at their parents.

'Life is so cruel,' Shaheen continued in a remorseful and thoughtful voice. Everything seemed clearer. She had developed a deep admiration and love for her parents, knowing how hard they had struggled over the years. She felt it was not right to give others an opportunity to talk badly of her parents, as she would if she disobeyed them.

'You just going to take it, then?' Jalib was unhappy once again. This time no tears rushed to his eyes, or Shaheen's. They knew tears would not help. Their bodies were filled with sadness. It seemed as though their love was dying in front of their eyes.

'Shall we run away together?' Jalib asked in a desperate voice. 'You used to joke about it. I'm really serious now.' Jalib was excited. If only she'd say yes now, they could go somewhere far away and leave all their worries behind. He looked deeply into her eyes, certain she would say yes, and then they would be happy together somewhere.

Shaheen went very quiet. If she went away she could avoid ever meeting Maqsood. No strange man would then put his arms round her. She could live a free life somewhere else, far away from her family. They could never trace her. These thoughts had often come to her. The temptation was great. So many times she had convinced herself that this was the only way and that the next morning she would pack her clothing and jump on a train to London and disappear into the glamour and glitter of that city. After all, Afshan and Amarjit, her two school-friends, had done so. Since they had left home, no one had heard of them. Their parents never talked about them. It was as though they had never existed. Amarjit's father had taken to drinking heavily; although he never talked about it to anyone, the reason why he had become an alcoholic was well known. He never recovered from the shock of his daughter leaving home. Amarjit's mother had gone back to India with her other two daughters, fearing that maybe they too would go the same way. Afshan's father had had a heart attack. Shaheen wondered if she could ever put her beloved parents through so much pain.

She saw herself sitting on a train bound for London, her problems being cut away in the rhythmic music of the train. Then she saw the corpses of her father and mother in front of her, the children sitting at home crying, with no one to greet them as they came back from their long journey to school. Her oldest brother had all but disappeared into oblivion.

Although Jalib sat in front of her, he seemed not to exist for her at that moment. He had always before, whenever she had suggested the possibility of leaving home, pretended not to hear. Today, it had come to her that perhaps all this time he had been thinking about it.

If she did run away now, she saw behind her her family, thrown into an eternity of misery. What about the children? What would they grow up thinking? That their sister had run away? She could never see them again, play with them, see the face of her mother or any of her loved ones. She felt as though she had already left home. She was filled with a monumental sadness. Torn through her soul. Every part of her body felt subjected to a physical torture.

'No, Jalib, I can't do that.' She thought how childish it was to think these things. 'We can't just run away from our problems.' She saw before her her *doli*, showered in a monsoon of her tears. 'For my happiness, I couldn't cause so much misery to my parents.' She felt a melancholy pang inside her as she spoke the words by which she felt she was sealing her life. The agony of it all had dried up. In its place now hung a reconciliation; although uneasy, it stood clearly before her. 'Whatever happens, I'm not going to become a *wohti* that easily!' A smile at last made an appearance on her lips. As she smiled, she noticed Jalib was shining with happiness beside her. She knew he didn't understand her last remarks, but that he was happy simply because he had seen her smile. She felt he couldn't really understand this sort of thing. She was beginning to harden in the face of all her problems. She was determined to find a way out. There had to be one, even at this late hour. She felt comforted, and with these thoughts she

108

pushed her worries to the back of her mind and started to talk about what had been discussed in this very room, following the attack on Malkit.

'You lads talk about so much. Yet you don't know what to do, do you?' She teased Jalib. After all their hot words they seemed to have forgotten about 'getting together'. 'If I could join in your meetings, I'd show you wind-bags!' She was angry that nothing had materialized from the discussions.

On many occasions, when she had seen a demonstration on the television news, she had longed to be with them, shouting about her life and the life of her people. But her solidarity had never reached beyond the surface of the television screen. She was determined that some day, when she felt strongly about something, she would join in the demonstration, no matter what her family said, no matter what anyone thought.

'It's not like that.' Jalib was now on the defensive. He realized that what Shaheen said was correct but he felt awkward not knowing what to do. 'We just haven't got together since that day.'

'And what of this revolutionary? I suppose he's stuck with those meetings of his,' she said with sarcasm, referring to Hussain, whom she didn't particularly like, as she felt he was just a talker. 'Can't he find any long words to explain why you lads can't do anything useful? The only one of you lot who makes any sense is Mo. At least he's honest.' She had had a long conversation with Mohan shortly after the attack on Malkit. He had explained to her that he was very keen on the idea of action but didn't know what to do. She had liked his sincerity. Whereas Hussain, she felt, thought he knew all the answers, but did nothing except sell papers.

'I've been talking a lot to Baba Dalair Singh lately. He's given me lots of ideas about how they used to do things in India,' Jalib replied, trying to give the impression that as far as he was concerned he had not given up the idea. 'I really like talking to him nowadays. I don't find him such a bore as I used to.'

Shaheen was pleased to hear Jalib talk like this. She got tired of talking about nothing but everyday things. This way she felt she could let out her innermost desires. She had never talked to Dalair Singh but lately she had heard a lot about him from Jalib.

She had once wanted to meet him but had decided against it in case he was a friend of her father.

'I can say one thing,' she said looking at her watch and realizing it was getting close to the time when she had to go home, 'whatever happens to my life, I'm not going to give up.' She did not know quite where these words came from but ever since they had started to talk of forming an organization, she had begun to relate many parts of her life to it. Before, she had seen her problem in isolation. Now, she was beginning to see it in relation to many other people.

'There's always got to be a way out. I mean, it's no bloody good just eating ourselves up, when these skinheads, coppers and others are doing so much wrong to us folk.' She continued to talk about what she felt was happening to her people. It would anger her so much that, whenever she talked about these things, Jalib would just nod in agreement. He was doing this now.

'Can't you say anything but only shake your stupid loaf,' she said with a smile. At this, Jalib flung himself at her and they both fell on the floor. 'You're such a kid,' she smiled, and kissed him. For a moment, her problems melted.

'When you do get this meeting going,' she said as she made herself ready to leave, 'make sure you tell me. I'll try to come along.'

'But there's going to be all those lads there,' Jalib protested, trying to say that she should not get involved in this sort of thing. 'After all, don't you think that you've got enough on your plate without making matters worse for yourself?' He felt certain of one thing: that whatever they discussed at the meeting, it was not the business of women. What would happen if they went somewhere and had a fight with skinheads, and she was there, he asked.

'You don't have to talk like my father as well. Things couldn't get any worse. I can look after myself.' She felt certain of one thing: that her life as a wife of Maqsood would not be completely in vain. She felt that there was so much to be done and there was so much she could do if only she had a chance. She would get very hurt when Jalib talked in this patronizing way, for she felt he was acting like her father and trying to protect her – from God knew what.

They didn't pursue this argument as there was not much time

left. They hugged each other closely and then Jalib went out of the house to see if anyone was around. Making sure no one saw her leave, he signalled to her and she promptly ran out of the house and past him.

On her way home, she had a frightening thought. 'What if I'm pregnant? Stupid girl! That's all you need now,' she said to herself, preparing herself for her return home. All else faded but her home and the need to act normally. She hoped Kiran hadn't forgotten that she was supposed to be with Shaheen.

She greeted her mother and went straight up to her room. There she jumped on her bed and started to relive the afternoon, its joys and its sadness.

Chapter 15

Rumours had been rife in Bradford that the National Front were going to hold a demonstration in Manningham. There was much apprehension and excitement among the people of the area. At first, there were just rumours and no one was quite sure what to make of them. After all, hadn't there been hundreds of rumours before, with nothing materializing? This was the general attitude.

But the day the local newspapers confirmed that the National Front were indeed going to march, the town seemed to light up. Suddenly everyone was talking about the danger, and an ad hoc committee against racism and fascism was formed. In the initial days, it was composed of various left-wing organizations. But soon local mosques, *gurdwaras* and temples joined in and with them came all the organizations of the black community.

Word also got around that some of the local *chamchas* had been meeting with the police, begging them not to allow the National Front to come to Bradford. The exact words and conversation between the police and these Uncle Toms will never be known, but they did not manage to get what they were after. They returned empty-handed and from that day never mentioned that the meeting had taken place.

The Ad Hoc Committee Against Racism and Fascism had organized a public meeting opposing the planned 'march' by the fascists. It was well-attended, with many people helping with door-to-door distribution of leaflets. Religious institutions had all started to work towards mobilization of people before the meeting. Although it was organized on short notice, the turn-out was impressive.

At the same time, the youth of the city had been talking about the coming 'march'. They were agreed: 'There's only one thing for it – let's smash the bastards!' Wherever youth gathered, this was invariably their attitude. So, while the professional activists were publicly debating whether fascists had the right to freedom of speech, the black youth from various national backgrounds were very clearly saying, 'Let them come – we must smash them!'

The platform of the public meeting was dominated by middle-aged Asian men, representing various religious and other organizations. No one knew all these groups existed but suddenly they had surfaced, with their representatives on the stage, making long speeches. Various left-wing groups present also put forward their points of view, some from the floor, others from the platform. All in all, the meeting was very animated.

The spokesman from the *gurdwara* stood on the platform. 'Comrades, we cannot let these racists come to our town. The Sikh community and the *gurdwaras* have sent telegrams to the Chief of Police, asking him to ban the demonstration.' His comments were greeted with loud applause from the floor. 'If he does not ban the march, we will be on the streets to protect our lives and our property. We have also sent a telegram to the Home Secretary, asking him to spare us from these racists. It looks like all our pleas have fallen on deaf ears. The Guru Nanak Gurdwara will be asking the Sikh community to come out on the day the National Front come here, to show our opposition by demonstrating. We are a peaceful people and we want a peaceful demonstration.' He sat down to loud applause.

And so it went on. Speaker after speaker went to the platform and said much the same thing as the one before him. The Home Secretary should ban the march and failing this, then the speaker's organization or religious institution would ask people to come out on to the streets on the day the fascists came to town.

A local white activist came forward. 'Comrades, my organization says that the fascists should not be given the right to freedom of speech.' Loud applause greeted him. 'We say, "Yes, ban the Front" – but be careful, the state will also ban us. Fascism is not just a threat to black people but to the whole of the labour movement.' After a short pause, he continued, 'The fascists say there are so many whites on the dole, kick out the blacks and there will be jobs for all whites. Now, that's a lie. There are hardly any blacks in Scotland. And yet unemployment there is about the highest there is in the country. So you see, they are just using you for scapegoats. And when they say that so many immigrants have entered the country, they don't tell us that more leave the country than come here. My organization says proudly, about the immigrants, "They are welcome here!" '

'Stop playing the numbers game, brother.' Hussain had been getting very irritated by the patronizing attitude of the speaker and exploded with this shout.

'Hear, hear,' a voice agreed from somewhere in the packed hall.

'Keep quiet,' thundered the chairman of the meeting, his voice echoing around the room. 'Please continue, sir.'

'I am happy to see so many black faces here today,' the speaker continued, 'but why are there so few young people here? The youth must also mobilize. Our organization has decided that it will mobilize all its northern branches. We say, "Black and White – Unite and Fight". Thank you comrade chairman and friends.'

As the white speaker finished, about a hundred youths walked into the meeting. From everywhere in the hall, loud clapping rang out. Hussain turned and waved to Jalib, who had come with the others. Apparently, they had been arguing among themselves as to whether they should participate in the meeting. Some of them raised objections to their participation on the grounds that they did not want to sit and listen to a load of rubbish churned out by *chamchas*. Others said that their fathers and uncles would be there, and so they might get into trouble. Finally, Jalib had won them to the position that they must all participate in the meeting as almost everyone representing anything would be there and if they all went in together they could not be ignored.

When the applause had died down, Jalib came to sit next to Hussain. Hussain felt a lot of confidence in himself, now that the youth would back him if he stood up to say anything.

'Comrades and brothers,' the chairman spoke loudly through the microphone, 'from the mood of the meeting . . .'

'Speak in Punjabi! At least let us understand what is going on,' Dalair Singh, who had been sitting very quietly through the proceedings, shouted across to the chairman.

'. . . that we don't want these racists to come to our town,' – the chairman at once switched to Punjabi – 'I know there are lots of young people here. You must listen. We want a peaceful demonstration. We don't want any violence. We are hoping that, in the next few days, the police will decide to ban the march and then we can go about our lives in peace again.'

'No! Smash the fascists! The police won't protect us! Don't rely on them!' Hussain impulsively shouted from his chair, to be

114

greeted by loud ululation from the youth, who stood menacingly at the back of the hall.

'Keep quiet, young man!' the chairman roared angrily, 'you're too young to understand these matters!'

'Don't insult me!' Hussain shouted back at the chairman. 'We must defend ourselves.' He was again greeted with animated cheering from the youth. The mass of the people in the meeting were getting bored with the speeches. And the boredom was now floating about the room in endless clouds of smoke. No sooner had Hussain spoken than the room was again full of life.

'Go on, brother Hussain! Get up there and do your thing, man!' A youth shouted from the back of the hall.

'Go on, get up on the stage, son!' someone else shouted.

'There is no time left for speakers.' The chairman felt that if he allowed Hussain to speak anything could happen. You can't let young blood get the better of you, he thought, worried that Hussain would make a speech about violent confrontation with the police, who would obviously be protecting the fascists.

'Let him speak,' another voice shouted angrily at the chairman. There was an uneasy feeling spreading across the hall. Jalib pushed Hussain to stand up. Hussain impulsively went to the front of the hall and, without looking at the chairman, picked up the microphone.

'Comrades, I've sat through all this meeting. Speaker after speaker – all saying we're peaceful people, please Mr Policeman, protect us. The police WON'T protect us! How can we be peaceful when fascists are killing our people? If they come here, we must smash them! Speakers asked the cops to ban the fascists. Let me tell you, they will also ban us. There was a white comrade – although he was trying to help us, in reality he insulted us. He played the game of the racists. I don't care if the whole of the subcontinent comes here. It is the wealth of our people that they have stolen from us over the centuries. It's not a favour to let us come here. It is our right!'

'Right on, brother,' Jalib shouted, filled with joy.

'Back in the thirties, in Cable Street, when the fascists planned to march in the East End of London, the people said, "They shall not pass." We too must say that they shall not pass. When the fascists come here, we must smash the scum!' Loud whistling and roaring broke out in the hall as Hussain continued to articulate the wishes of the people and of the youth.

'Someone talked about freedom of speech. We will not give someone the freedom to go around inciting violence against our people. Nor the freedom to kill our people. I say, Smash the Front! Death to Fascism!' Hussain stopped, his blood bouncing in his temples. He left the platform to a standing ovation.

'Good, brother!' Jalib patted Hussain on the back; Hussain was trying to calm himself by inhaling deeply the smoke from his cigarette.

'Comrades and brothers,' the chairman continued, trying to undercut the impact of what Hussain had just said. He was filled with apprehension, in case rioting broke out and his shop would be caught up in the looting. 'After the next speaker, from the Hindu temple, who is also on the Ad Hoc Committee Against Racism and Fascism, I will close the meeting.'

'Comrades,' the speaker from the temple began, 'we from the Hindu temple, and I speak on behalf of the Hindu community, also feel that the Home Office should ban the Front from marching here.' And so he continued, with much the same thing as all the other representatives. 'The committee has worked out a route for our demonstration. Shortly we will be issuing leaflets in all ethnic languages. Let us make our demonstration on the twenty-third a success. As the secretary of the Committee, I would like to thank everyone for coming. Bring your friends and relatives on the twenty-third. Thank you for coming, brothers and sisters.'

As people left, the chairman announced that funds were needed for the demonstration and those present were invited to give donations to the stewards waiting, with buckets, at the door.

Although Hussain had attended all the meetings of the Ad Hoc Committee, he held no official position. When the route of the anti-fascist march had been discussed, he had argued strongly that it should remain in Manningham, as that was the area the fascists were likely to march in. The majority of the elders had argued that this would lead to confrontation with the police, while their objective was to show the white people that, although they felt strongly about the National Front, they were still law-abiding. On a few occasions, Hussain had been stopped from arguing his position, on the basis that he was not a delegate from any organization. The reason he was allowed to remain in the meetings was that the Committee felt that it was necessary to have some young people on it. A few times Jalib and Mohan had accompanied him, sitting silently, boredom often driving them out of the meetings.

Eventually a route was agreed with the police. The anti-fascist demonstration was to start in the Infirmary Fields at the end of Lumb Lane. After going up into Manningham, it would come back down Lumb Lane, cut across the Manningham Lane and end at the Tyrlls outside the Central Police Station. No one was certain where the National Front were going to assemble. The police had kept that a tightly guarded secret between themselves and the fascists.

A few days before the demonstration was due to be held, someone had gone into the Infirmary Fields, under cover of darkness and sprayed graffitti all over one of the walls – 'NAZIS OUT', 'FASCIST SCUM', and so on. Judging by the way it was written, it was obvious the person was in a hurry – in one place, the word 'FASCIST' was misspelled. Symbolically, it was a big boost for the people who gathered in the Infirmary Fields to march against the fascist threat.

At one of Hussain's union meetings, Ghulam B. Azad had moved a motion that they should support the demonstration with union funds and also mobilize all the workers from the mill. Although some of the white workers had argued that they should not bring politics into the union meetings, it had been passed by a majority of the workers who had attended. From here on, Hussain and Azad spent much of their spare time trying to mobilize the workers for the anti-fascist demonstration.

The day before the demonstration, the whole town was buzzing with excitement. The police had made statements to the press and media that, in their opinion, the National Front posed no threat to public order, and therefore they had not applied to the Home Secretary for a ban on all demonstrations.

On Friday, as the faithful went to the mosques to pray, the mullahs, after each session, asked the congregation to come to the demonstration, saying it was their duty to oppose racism and fascism. The *gurdwara* and the temple had likewise been calling upon their faithful to come out on to the streets, as there was no other way of living in peace. The local Trades' Council had agreed to send its banner for the demonstration.

All in all, the organization of the community had come together in a united front to oppose the march on Bradford. Everywhere, wherever there was room for a poster, people were called to oppose fascism and support the counter-demonstration.

The local newspaper, in line with the police, had advised its readers to keep away from the city centre and from Manningham on the twenty-third. Some shopkeepers closed their shops early, anticipating trouble. Others had put up posters supporting the demonstration, thereby hoping to attract the demonstrators for business.

At midday on the twenty-third, the banner of the Ad Hoc Committee Against Racism and Fascism arrived in Infirmary Fields, accompanied by about twenty people. Slowly, people trickled in. A few police vans were keeping a close eye on the gathering. Then, without apparent reason, the vans emptied and the police came into the Fields and formed a long line, in twos. They slowly marched towards the demonstrators, who by now numbered a few hundred. As they set foot in the Fields, they were greeted by loud whistling and shouting from the people. They stopped about thirty yards away from the people and spread out in a single line, neatly. They were then joined by more police who stood in fours at regular intervals behind the first line. The reason for their move soon became clear. Just above the heads of the long line of police Union Jacks could be seen. The National Front had arrived under heavy escort. At the sight of the Union Jack, people who had gathered in the Fields and who by now numbered thousands, surged forward. Stewards from the Ad Hoc Committee spread out to stop people from going further. The air filled with anger and chants.

'Comrades, comrades,' shouted a steward down his megaphone, in an animated voice, 'this is obviously a police trick to get us to attack the Front here, so that our demonstration won't take place. We will demonstrate and make this day a success!' His voice was drowned by chants of 'Nazi scum off our streets! Nazi scum off our streets!'

A group of youths ran towards the police lines with some missiles and hurled them at the fascists over the heads of the police and then ran back to the safety of the crowd. Unknown to the chanting mass, people carrying the Trades' Council banner were attacked as they made their way towards the Infirmary

Fields. While everyone's attention was focused on the fascists who had entered the Fields behind the police, a small group of fascists, who had been lingering amongst the Saturday shoppers, had seen the Trades' Council banner come along the road. Realizing that they had greater numbers, they attacked the Trades' Council and, although none of the people attacked received any serious injuries, the very old banner of the Trades' Council was torn and ripped to shreds.

Back in the Fields, Jalib and Mohan were jumping up and down, in rhythm with the chants. Jalib's eyes filled with hatred as he saw the symbol of the enemy, the Union Jack, waving above the sea of deep blue. He wanted the demonstration to charge at the police lines and attack the fascists, before they could march. He could not understand why, when the objective of the demonstration was to stop the fascists from marching, they should just stand around, when the fascists were within reach. Unable to move on his own, he let out his frustration in loud chants.

By now, the chairman of the Committee was talking to the police officer a few yards from the mass of the people, accompanied by a large delegation from the Ad Hoc Committee.

'Officer, this is outrageous! If you do not move the National Front away from this place immediately, I cannot guarantee control of the demonstration. Can't you see the people are getting angrier every second?'

'I'm not a politician,' replied the officer in a cool voice. It was as if he wanted a reaction from the people. 'They have just as much right as you to hold a peaceful demonstration. However, I will see their organizers and ask them to start their march.'

'Sir, why have you allowed the National Front to assemble here at the same time and place as us?' asked the chairman, bewildered. The officer turned his back and disappeared behind the blue line, which was now three deep and stretching the whole width of the Infirmary Fields.

Within minutes, the Union Jacks started to move, surrounded by hundreds of police. On either side of the National Front, there was a line two deep of police. In front of the fascist march a police van slowly moved along the roads. Behind it, two mounted policemen rode. To protect the rear of the fascist march, police had provided a cavalcade of vans and four mounted men.

This large police protection offered to the fascists drowned

119

them in a sea of deep blue. The large numbers of police were prominent in their organized march and it was as if the Union Jacks and their flag-bearers were not the real marchers. It looked as if this was a police march. The fascists could hardly be seen. Only their flags waved in the wind, over the heads of the marching lines of the police.

As the fascists began to pull out of the Infirmary Fields, the crowd chanted louder and louder, taunting. When they were out of sight, the police withdrew from the Fields and their slow, orderly withdrawal was accompanied by the united chants of the people. Within a few minutes, the anti-fascist march was on the move. As it progressed through the streets, it grew in size.

'Black and White, Unite and Fight – Smash the National Front,' would ring out over the demonstration, followed by 'Death to Fascism'. At times, it was difficult to make out what the demonstrators were shouting.

Jalib shouted alongside his friends, who had all somehow managed to get together in the middle of the demonstration. His body filled with strength that came from the thousands of people shouting angrily at the fascists and the authorities who protected them. Looking at the sights of the familiar, run-down area, he felt as though it had at last come to life. It was the same area, but right now he felt that it had given birth to a long-expected but dormant power. He would see a friend and wave him to join the demonstration; and when he did, the youths would shout even louder, to let the whole world know that their numbers had increased. Jalib hadn't noticed that Dalair Singh had joined them and was awkwardly marching alongside them, as though his body had been filled with the fire of youthfulness all over again. Dalair's movements were awkward, but they were energetic.

No one quite knew what was going on. Some people said that the fascists were still in Manningham, others said that the police had brought them back to Infirmary Fields, and that they were assembling properly now the anti-fascists had moved out. With this cloud of confusion hanging over it, the demonstration moved noisily along the roads.

Slowly, it reached the centre of the town. The noise of the chants trapped in the tall buildings haunted the streets of the city centre with menace. All the shoppers stopped, aghast. All heads turned towards the chants of the march of the anti-fascists. Office workers, who had to work, peeped out of the windows and shop assistants stopped what they were doing, looking at each other or going to vantage points and staring at the mass of people walking by.

The faces of the Ad Hoc Committee Against Racism and Fascism smiled, contented, as the demonstration reached its conclusion, that the march had after all been peaceful. Outside the police station, the Committee had installed a public announcement system. As the demonstration reached its rallying point, a large group of youths began to assemble, just on the corner of the steps leading to the Magistrates' Court. Jalib stood at the top of the steps, his eyes fixed on the banners and crowds pouring towards the Tyrlls. Soon the whole area was full of people, and the crowd spilled over into the main road. At the sight of all these people Jalib swelled with pride and strength. He began to think about the Union Jacks, surrounded by all the police, guiding the fascists through the streets of Manningham.

'This is not right!' Dalair Singh spoke over the noise of the slogans of the people who were still arriving. 'The National Front won't come here. They're in Manningham!' Jalib had been thinking that there was something wrong about this demonstration. Dalair's words finally cleared his mind. It was Manningham that had to be defended! That was where the fascists were right then!

'What are we doing here?' Jalib shouted at the youths. 'The Front's in our streets! That's where we ought to be!'

The youths roared their agreement. The small group on the steps had now grown to a few hundred. Jalib looked towards the rostrum where there was a lot of commotion on the platform. A youth had frantically run down into town from Manningham and was demanding the microphone. The fascists were marching along Lumb Lane and everyone there was extremely frightened. When his request was refused, he snatched the microphone from the chairman's hands and hurriedly began shouting down it, 'The fascists are marching on Lumb Lane. What are we all doing here? If you want to defend your community, go to Lumb Lane!'

Amidst the gathering rally, there was a sudden movement. The contingent of youths smashed their way through the stewards who tried to stop them. They broke away from the rally, shouting and whistling hysterically. Jalib looked around him. He was surrounded by his friends. Together with the rest, they ran up

121

Godwin Street. At the top, a group of about twelve police blocked their path.

'Go back! Go back,' a policeman shouted down his megaphone at the angry mob driving at him like a mighty juggernaut. They were trying to make their way to the Manningham Middle School at the junction of Lumb Lane and Manningham Lane. Someone had said that, as soon as the youths had broken away from the rally the fascists had been rushed into the school.

'Shall we go another way?' asked a youth standing paralysed in front of the police line, not knowing what to do. Hussain, who was covered with sweat from the excitement and fear, suddenly burst out shouting, 'Death to fascism! Death to fascism!' Immediately, the rest of the youths started to chant after Hussain. Then they stopped. There was a massive feeling of indecisiveness in the air. The police moved, as if they were going to charge. The mob, as though pulled from behind by an invisible force, stepped back. Then silence. The faces of the police were filled with apprehension.

'There are only twelve pigs here, brothers!' shouted Jalib as he pushed his way to the front of the crowd, speaking in Punjabi so they could not understand him. 'If you want to smash the Front, go through the pigs. Come on, brothers! There are only twelve of them!' A roar rang out from the assembled youths. They charged the police who immediately ran down towards the centre of the town.

Running past bewildered Saturday shoppers, Hussain felt angry with himself. At such a critical moment, when he should have provided leadership to the youths, all he could do was shout slogans at the police. He cursed all the time he had spent in his organization. In all that time, he had learnt only to shout slogans, even when his town was being held at the mercy of the police and the fascists.

Breaking through the police line, some youths shouted that they should chase the pigs, but the vast majority ran towards the school without looking back. Running through the stationary traffic, Jalib was ecstatic about the victory over the police. It had given him even more energy and courage. The hysterical mob ran towards Infirmary Fields, breaking at random into smaller groups and then joining up again.

Jalib glanced occasionally at Mohan. He was also totally caught up in the electrified atmosphere of their resistance to the threat of fascism. As he ran with the others, he thought how the same surroundings, which even yesterday had filled him with boredom and listlessness and frustration, now were charged with an energy he had never seen before. He felt as if the buildings along their path were saluting him on their mission. Cautiously, driving some distance behind the crowd, a police van kept a keen eye on them. Although it had been following them, the police had not tried to make any arrests. It was obvious that the group running towards the school would vent their anger on the police if provoked in the slightest.

'I just seen *Baba* Dalair Singh behind us,' Jalib shouted to Hussain, who was now running next to him. 'The old man's come to join us!' Jalib felt a very strong feeling of affection towards Dalair Singh grow in him.

'The old man's a fighter, brother,' Hussain replied as they were swept along.

As the first few youths reached Manningham Middle School, they slowed down. A large group of West Indian youths had already congregated outside the Lumb Lane end of the school. Soon there were many hundreds of youths standing in the streets surrounding the school. They were joined by local residents.

A group of about fifty police guarded the back entrance of the school. The youths began to get restless. Someone started to whistle. The rest joined in. A loud ululation rang out across the whistling and shouting, like the roar of a lion before it pounced on its prey.

'Death to the National Front! Death to the National Front!' Everyone joined in. The chant roared across the house tops, bouncing off the walls of the school. Delair Singh rested his bulky frame on the grass, exhausted by his journey from the town centre. He was too old to run around like a young man, he thought. Yet still he wanted to show his rejection of the treachery of the so-called leaders of the community.

'Reactionary dogs,' he muttered, amidst the clapping, whistling and shouting of the youths. 'The fascists are in our streets and they lead the people into the town centre miles away. Just like Gandhi – the people were run down by the tanks and he still preached that they should peacefully sit in their way.'

'Brothers' – a Pakistani policeman walked forward from behind the lines of police guarding the fascists; he spoke in Urdu, trying

123

to convince the youths that he too was a part of their people – 'let the forces of law and order deal with the National Front. Go home peacefully now.' As he spoke, there was a loud noise of disgust. Someone broke a window in the post office. A brick flew from somewhere amongst the infuriated youths and landed in the face of the Pakistani policeman. Blood rushed from his nose. He stumbled forward. As he fell, his fall was greeted by enthusiastic applause. Two mounted police charged the crowd and two others picked up their injured comrade. The crowd scattered, and a hail of bricks and wood showered the police line.

The mounted police drew their long truncheons and charged the crowd, occasionally hitting someone on the shoulders or head. Police guarding the school withdrew in an orderly fashion behind the school wall. The injured Pakistani policeman had been hurriedly packed into an ambulance and it was now speeding towards the hospital with its beacon flashing. A full-scale pitched battle was in progress between the youths and the police. A police car was overturned. Someone set it on fire. Every time the police charged the youths would disperse and regroup, then attack the police with whatever they could lay their hands on. The police were determined that the fascists' meeting, taking place in the school amidst this battle, would not be stopped. The youths were showing their determination to get the fascists out of their area. It was apparent to them that if they wanted the fascists out of the school, they would first have to go through the lines of police protection.

In town, meanwhile, the rally was caught in a confusing mess of speeches. The chairman had repeatedly told the gathering that the youths were being irresponsible and that his organization did not have anything to do with them. Some speakers had urged the rally not to go towards Manningham as the demonstration had proved its point that people were opposed to the National Front.

The chairman was bringing the rally to a close. In the background, police sirens could be heard ringing across the approaching evening. 'We said we would protest against the National Front. We have done that. I cannot understand why the police would not ban the Front's demonstration. It is now too late for us to control the youth. Please go home.' His concluding speech was greeted with embarrassed silence.

Before the youths had broken away from the rally, all the

various left-wing groups had quite happily shouted their slogans. Not for one moment had any of them suggested that the demonstration should head back towards Manningham. But on seeing others going to protest in Manningham, some of them walked there in twos and threes. While the youths engaged the police in a pitched battle on the other side of the school, the people from these organizations sat down in the middle of Manningham Lane and began to sing in unison, 'We shall not be moved.' The mounted police charged and they moved. There was a heavy guard of police at the front entrance of the school and, behind the police, volunteers from the Territorial Army stood as a reserve.

When it was obvious the police could not hold the youths back much longer, the National Front were quickly shepherded into their coaches. As they left, towards the town centre, they were given a last farewell of a hail of missiles from those who had not managed to get through to the main body engaging the police.

Long after the Front left, the battle raged. As darkness fell, the police withdrew. The youths had, all but a few, gone home. The only reminder of the afternoon's battle were two smouldering police vehicles in the background, and broken and looted shops. Everyone's individuality had blended to a single mass of resistance, to a mob, unpredictable and explosive. Today's incidents changed the lives of the young people who had taken part in the fight, unselfishly, to protect their people from the menace of fascism.

Chapter 16

Hussain had left the International Socialists when the Somage splinter group was formed. A debate had begun to rage over the status of black workers in the organization, coupled with a general disillusionment of the black members. All the contradictions came to a head when the IS sacked its national race organizer. Although the demand for a black caucus was upheld, the full-time organizer was not reinstated.

The flickering flames of discontent coalesced in the Somage group. Hussain had not been very clear about the crux of the argument, but over the past few months he had felt a lot of frustration with his membership of the organization. After talking with Jalib and his friends, Hussain began to appreciate that all the time he had spent in the IS had estranged him from his people. He saw that the main interest of organizations of the left was not for the welfare of his people, but for the furtherance of the particular organization. If the group had a different priority, the plight of black people was dropped. He attended the first meeting of the Somage group, but since then he had lost interest. He felt that they were still really the same organization but operating under a different name. It was as though the barriers which kept Hussain away from his community had been taken over intact by Somage and placed around that faction too.

From time to time, Hussain had met with old friends who were either members of various other parties, or had been. Usually they had argued about the correctness of this line or that. But lately they had all talked of the one thing they had in common: all of them felt alienated from their community and felt a need for an organization involving their own community. In the past, because of their respective memberships of the Labour Party, the Militants, or the Workers' Revolutionary Party, or a multitude of other groups, they had regarded each other as class enemies. At last they had begun to talk about race and racism. They had agreed that the sectarian divide between them was a hindrance to the development of the organization they all wanted and the community needed.

The eruption on the streets, and the betrayal of the community by the *chamchas*, finally pushed them into a position where they agreed to discuss their differences openly and honestly and see if they could find enough common ground to be able to work together.

'Comrades,' Hussain opened the discussion, 'now that the dust has settled from the confrontation with the police, I think we must talk more seriously than we have in the past. On the twenty-third our "leaders" led us up a blind alley. If the whole demonstration had actually tried to come here to Manningham, instead of just the youth taking on the police, there is no doubt in my mind that the fascists would have well and truly got a hammering.'

There was an atmosphere of seriousness in Hussain's room amongst the handful of youths gathered there. Although all had left their respective organizations, they still clung to what they had learned through their politicization.

'I'm not clear on many things,' Hussain continued. 'I'm no theoretician, but I'm certain of one thing. It is time to launch a genuine organization of our youth.' He explained his view at great length, and it was obvious he had spent a great deal of time thinking about what he was saying. Although he admitted he was not clear on many things, Hussain felt that he could not wait until everything was crystal clear.

'I'm sure all of us feel the same way. But those points that aren't clear now have to become so as we struggle. We've all spent so much time and energy building these white left groups. What for? What have they done for us?'

The gathering sat quietly and listened. No one disagreed. Everyone shared this basic view.

Jeeta came into the discussion. 'It's good that at last we're moving in a direction where we can develop our own organization.' He too felt isolated and useless, both when he had been involved with the Militant Tendency, and especially since he had left. 'I share your views, Hussain. I personally feel that it is good that, even at this elementary stage, we are from different Asian communities. It is my opinion that it's necessary to form an Asian organization that cuts across all barriers.'

'You're right, Jeeta,' Harjosh, who had been itching to speak, replied with animation. 'Should we not perhaps be talking in terms of an Afro-Asian youth organization?' A heated debate developed on whether, from the outset, they should go for an Afro-Asian movement or a strictly Asian one. Finally, agreement was reached: they would form an Asian youth movement initially and would discuss the possibility of working in a common organization of black youth in the near future.

'Although I agree with Harjosh that it is necessary for all black people to unite in a common organization, let's face it, right now our own house is in such a mess that we'd better start by sorting it out.' Jeeta tried to conclude the discussion of this subject.

They talked at length about the demonstration on the twenty-third. They thought something disturbing had developed. The physical arrangement of the demonstration was such that all Muslims marched together as a contingent, all Sikhs marched as another, and Hindus as another. There were occasions when Muslims shouted their religious slogans and Sikhs replied with theirs.

'Man, it was touch and go for a while. I thought we were going to have a bloody punch-up!' Hussain laughed at his own words. Others smiled politely.

'What is important is that our communities were united in their stand against fascism,' Harjosh spoke, pointing to the fact that it was stupid and wrong to denigrate the people. 'Unity in action is important, not the slogan-mongering of a few.'

So the discussion went, sometimes going over points already covered, sometimes opening up new areas. They discussed the basic aims and objectives of the group they were trying to form. It was at this point that their differences began to come out into the open. When they started to talk about immigration, Hussain said that in his opinion they should not recognize the label of 'illegal immigrant'. He felt that black people had a right to come to this country by virtue of their history, the colonization of their lands and the enslavement of their peoples by Britain, and to live here free of restraints and harassment. Harjosh disagreed. Although he accepted in principle what Hussain was saying, he thought it was necessary to gain respectability first before talking publicly about these things. 'After all, we're not trying to build a communist party, you know!' He continued, reinforcing his position, 'By stating openly that in our view there is no such thing as an illegal immigrant, we are alienating ourselves from our people from the very beginning.'

The reason Hussain stuck so adamantly to his position was not so much that he had formed it as a result of serious thought and study but because so many of his own family were included in the term 'illegal immigrant' and he himself was not sure of his own 'legality'. He had long ago begun to question the merits of the term and now he thought it was dehumanizing to his people. He had begun to understand that this was a method of institutionalizing racism into the very heart of the state machinery.

Others agreed with him and Harjosh reluctantly, for the sake of unity, agreed to accept the majority view of the people in the room.

Some time earlier, Jeeta and his friends had already tried to form a youth organization. Although Jeeta had argued very strongly that they should form an organization embracing all the Asian community he had been defeated. Thereafter the organization was known as the Indian Progressive Youth Association.

'It is important that we learn some lessons from the IPYA,' Jeeta insisted. He went on to explain why the Association had not succeeded in winning the support of the young. 'The main reason for its quick downfall was that the Indian Workers' Association, Comrade Joshi's one, thought that their rivals in the other Indian Workers' Association were forming a youth wing, so they mobilized in force. I tell you, the executive committee of the IPYA were all over forty. Perhaps someone should have told them that the other IWA didn't even know about the meeting.'

Everyone laughed, but they all agreed that the organization they were trying to build must, at all costs, safeguard its independence from any of the established groups.

They moved on from the fear of their community's organizations pressuring them to become a youth wing to the very real threat of infiltration by various left-wing groups.

'We can safeguard ourselves simply by putting a condition on membership that no one should be a member of any other organization.' Hussain thought that as soon as they declared themselves publicly various groups would start to send their Asian members to the meetings. 'After all, we used to do that kind of dirty work all those years, recruiting and so on. The

129

white left-wing groups haven't changed, nor are they likely to.'

Darkness had crept into the streets. They had been so engrossed in their discussions they had lost all idea of time. Although there had been no agreed agenda, the discussion had been such that an agenda had emerged: the need for an organization, its orientation, its aims and objectives – at least some of the major points – and how to maintain its independence.

'Should we not, perhaps, have involved Jalib, Mohan and their friends in this meeting?' Harjosh asked. He had not said much during the meeting and his question was not specifically aimed at anyone. He thought it would have been wise to involve others in their first discussions. After all, the organization was going to consist of them.

'We've had a few chats,' Hussain replied. 'Those lads are with us all the way. I feel we should sort out a few positions and organizational questions first. Once we have a basis for elementary unity and organization, we can go and ask them to join us.' His basic point was, that in order to involve the broadest possible layer of youth, it was necessary to have the politically conscious comrades united first and then lay a basis for disciplined discussion to take place, out of which an organization could be born, with united leadership.

The meeting concluded. A thick blanket of smoke hung heavily over the room. Their bodies ached with fatigue and their eyes watered from the effect of the smoke.

Jeeta accepted responsibility for preparing a written document of the aims and objectives, based on what had been discussed, to be ready for the next meeting.

The time and place for the next meeting was arranged. They agreed they would meet in two days, at the same time, in Hussain's room.

'After we've sorted out these aims and objectives,' Jeeta said as he stood up to leave, 'we can go all out for a mass meeting and elect an executive committee.'

After everyone left, Hussain went straight to bed. He had only a few hours left to grab some sleep. Feeling happy that at last things were moving, he fell asleep with thoughts of talking to Jalib, Mohan and the others.

When he learned of the arrangements for forming an Asian youth movement, Mohan talked excitedly to Jalib. For the past

130

week, he had been in Southall, visiting relatives. He had met people there from the Southall Youth Movement and had spent many hours at their centre.

'It isn't really much to look at,' Mohan said, 'but at least it was a place where the kids could go.' He told Jalib that shortly after the formation of SYM they had acquired a building. 'I think they looked around for a building for some time and then just squatted in number twelve.'

'Go on, then,' Jalib almost shouted, feeling a quiet pride that they had taken something and not grovelled to get it. Apparently the building in which the SYM had squatted belonged to a local Indian businessman. After a few weeks arguing, with him and the local Council, the SYM had been granted a licence. As the businessman was one of the so-called community leaders, he felt that, unless he showed some concern and let the SYM have the building for a nominal rent, his standing in the community would be adversely affected. Like any businessman, however, he also saw the financial benefits of the SYM renovating the building. He had his eyes on the presidency of the Southall Indian Workers' Association, and he felt that in the long run this would be a good gimmick to win votes. For all intents and purposes, the Southall Indian Workers' Association was as institutionalized as the machinery of the state.

'Man, I tell you,' Mohan continued, talking about what he had seen, 'those guys seem to be getting money from all over the place.' He was excited about the thought of something similar happening here.

Jalib listened patiently as Mohan explained that there were quite a few youth groups in the south, all managing to acquire some money from somewhere or in the process of getting money. From the way he talked, one got the impression that no sooner had a youth group been formed than they started to receive money from various agencies.

Mohan was anxious to talk to Hussain and others who were running around trying to form the Asian Youth Movement, to tell them about what he had learnt from his visit to Southall. 'We could do with a centre here,' he continued, 'a pool table and things like that. At least we'll have somewhere to go and do things.'

'Yeah, but I thought we were getting this thing together so that we could go on demonstrations and things like that,' Jalib said, a bit unclear about what would happen if they tried to get a centre. But he didn't spend much time on these thoughts.

'You still can, can't you?' Mohan replied, in an argumentative tone. 'Maybe you should see their place, then you'd feel okay.' He could not understand why Jalib did not like what he had described.

'I suppose you're right,' Jalib ended the discussion.

That evening, Mohan went to see Hussain and explain what he had seen. He was pleased that Hussain approved what he described.

'At least wait until we're on our feet, brother! Once we get our executive committee, we'll have to send someone down to Southall to see what these guys are about.' Already Hussain saw the prospect of some sort of national link with various youth groups that were springing up around the country.

And so it continued. Long animated discussions were taking place among the youth about what they could do when they were organized. Hussain, Harjosh and Jeeta agreed to draft the aims and objectives that Jeeta had written out: opposition to racism, opposition to fascism, opposition to all forms of discrimination based on race, colour or religion: promotion of the interests of the peoples of the Indian subcontinent in cultural, social and political areas; support for all genuine national liberation movements; support and encouragement of Afro-Caribbean youth in similar organizations. Although there had been no disagreement on the issue of national liberation movements, they had been apprehensive about how other youth would react. Membership of the organization was to be open to all people under the age of thirty-five who originated from the Indian subcontinent.

They would put these aims and objectives to the mass meeting for approval, an executive committee would be elected and it would run the organization on a day-to-day basis.

Chapter 17

The stillness of the night was broken with the monotonous cries of the mill. Its blood-sucking refrain roared across the skies to melt with the sound of other machinery, singing out from all directions.

As usual, workers on the night shift looked anxiously at the clock that hung uncaring at the end of one of the aisles, willing its hands to move to six o'clock, when the machines would be switched off. And when this happened, the mill was engulfed in an eerie silence, as though the machines detested the fact that their slaves could just turn them off, sit and rest.

Some workers would sit in the canteen. Others, too exhausted to make the trip, although it was only a few yards away, would arrange the bobbins full of thread in such a manner that they could rest on them, using larger containers of yarn as pillows. They would stretch themselves out and feel the tiredness and exhaustion from their hours of enslavement move down from their necks, through their spinal cords, along their legs and blissfully out through their feet, on to the floor and into the stationary machines.

Ever since his confrontation with the management over the wage rise Ghulam B. Azad had felt bitterness and resentment at what he saw as a total betrayal by the regional organizer. Although he had been tempted to hit him, Ghulam had restrained himself, knowing such a move would result in instant dismissal.

When he lived in Pakistan, long before he came to England, Ghulam had once worked in a factory. Whenever the events leading up to the betrayal by the regional organizer crossed his mind, he would think about that time and the confrontation in which he had been involved with the owners of the factory there. There, he had witnessed a similar situation. A prominent politician had come to the factory and said much the same things as the regional organizer. On that day, the workers had been persuaded to go back to work, but it was not long before they saw through

133

the conniving moves of the politician. The factory was one of the few in which the union was allowed, and the union man had behaved just like the regional organizer. However, the shop stewards had managed to win the workers' agreement to a position where they could *gherao* the management, and thus they were in the end able to win their demands.

Ghulam had seen too many such betrayals of workers not to feel bitter. But, even so, he did not lose heart. He had long ago resolved to fight for whatever he thought was just. It was this determination which kept him in a mood to support his fellow-workers, whenever any of them was faced with some problem at work, or whenever they were feeling down. It was precisely because of his caring and love for his fellow-workers that they respected him so much.

After the incident over the wage demand, he did not allow himself to insult his fellow-workers, but instead patiently explained what had transpired and what they should have done. In fact, after that incident, he managed to win the night-shift workers to the position that, in the future, they would deal with their grievances themselves, and, even if none of them had a good command of English, they would still not let someone else do the talking for them.

When Hussain began working at the mill, Ghulam had been very pleased. He hoped, at last, that they would be able to air their views through one of their own workers. Still, Hussain was new and could not be thrown into the middle of a struggle that would jeopardize his position at the mill. And Ghulam B. Azad felt that there were many things Hussain still had to learn. These were the thoughts going through his head as he lay stretched out on the makeshift bed of thread and yarn, fending off the tempting approaches of sleep.

'So they are going to lay off some of us, at last.' The jobber who was well in with the management spoke, as he pushed a large basket away from himself. 'The overlooker told me that they are going to bring in new machinery and that one in three workers will be laid off.'

Hearing this, the rest of the workers snapped out of sleep and drowsiness, feeling pangs of fear shoot through their bodies, seeing before their eyes the disappearance of their livelihood. The jobber continued to explain what he had learnt. For some time now, management had been considering the introduction of labour-saving machinery.

'Of course,' the jobber continued in an indifferent tone, 'they will be paying redundancies to all those who deserve it. We have to move with the times, you know.' The meaning of his tone was very clear to the rest of the workers. They understood that he had been guaranteed his own job and he was trying to cushion the blows that were to fall on the other workers.

Ghulam looked up from his bed. He saw in the jobber all the qualities that made the regional organizer into the man he was. 'Here we are, about to lose our jobs, and he's trying to make us feel grateful to the company,' he thought with resentment. He too had heard this news, but had said nothing as this sort of rumour was rife everywhere now that the textile industry was caught in the grip of the slump.

'Surely we shouldn't just accept this, brother,' said a worker, turning nervously to Ghulam, his eyes eager, wondering if there was anything that could be done to safeguard their jobs and livelihoods.

'Don't worry, brother Mazaffer,' Ghulam replied, in a reassuring voice. The workers looked pained. For years they had given patient and loyal service to the company which was now going to lead them to the dole queues. All the injustice they had endured at work seemed to be in vain. 'If we all stick together and get the lads from the day shift with us as well, we can fight them and win.' These words fell like water on someone who has just crossed a lonely desert. Although Ghulam had replied to Mazaffer, his answer sounded like sweet music to the rest of the workers. They then sat up and talked at length about why it was so essential for all the workers to be united.

'The *goras* won't come with us,' Mazaffer said, pointing out that wherever the white workers acted in unity with the blacks, it was a deceitful trick in which they were conniving with management. 'You know that, brother, don't you?' From the way Mazaffer spoke, it was obvious he had apprehensions about support from the white workers. As all the white workers were in supervisory jobs, their positions would be safeguarded. So it was clear to everyone that they would not unite with the black workers, who would therefore face the axe alone.

'Let's not worry about that,' Ghulam said. He agreed with

Mazaffer but was still certain that, if they took action, the more unity they could build among the work-force, the more power they would have. 'After all, 90 per cent of the workers in this mill are our people. If the *goras* come with us, alright. If they don't, then they're against us and we fight them as well!'

The jobber sat without saying anything, listening to every word that was said. His hawkish eyes were sharply focused on Ghulam. Although he was aware that the jobber could not be trusted, Ghulam continued talking without any worry, knowing it would soon all be out in the open anyway.

The tea break had ended long ago but no one took any notice. They continued to plan what they should do. The spinning department, where they were now meeting, was packed with workers from other departments of the mill.

As Ghulam B. Azad spoke about how hard the coming battle would be, he was filled with joy at seeing his fellow-workers united. This gave him more encouragement and convinced him that, if all the workers united, they would not lose. This time, he did not have any doubts. The regional organizer for the union had to be avoided. He was thinking that, once all the workers had agreed a plan of action, they would approach the national union and enlist its support. If that failed, they would have to go directly to the shop floor of other factories and mills to get support from other workers.

The night shift stayed behind to meet the day shift and get their views. At eight thirty, about an hour before the management arrived, they started their first meeting. Almost every worker was present. The overlookers stood huddled together in a corner, frightened at the large number of workers gathered. There was anger everywhere. Years of hard work had brought workers to a position where they had to make a stand. There was no other way to solve their problem.

Standing on an overturned drum, Ghulam started talking in Punjabi.

'We know that a lot of us are going to get the boot. All the night-shift workers have met and all of us feel that there is only one way to deal with a situation like this. We will not, and cannot, accept any one of us getting the sack.' This was greeted with applause.

'If we have ever had to have unity, this is the time. The last

136

time we asked for a wage rise, we were sold out. They scared us by the threat of a life on the dole. You know, brothers, they always come up with something with which to put fear into us, whenever we try to resist. This time we have nothing to lose. They can't say that we might lose our jobs – they're sacking us anyway! Mark my words, it is only the beginning. They will eventually kick every one of us out if they can get away with it!' As Ghulam spoke, the will to resist and struggle in unity radiated across the floor of the room and bounced off the stationary machinery, mockingly. The atmosphere of the room contained a spirit of resistance.

'Brother Hussain, you should say what I have said in English, so that our white brothers can understand as well. Today, we'll conduct this meeting in our own language.' Ghulam pointed to Hussain who had been totally engrossed in what was being said.

During the time of the workers' last wage demand, the regional organizer's role had left Hussain feeling helpless. Since the time he had started working at the mill, he had gone through many changes in his thinking. In the time he had been with the International Socialists, he had built a very romantic picture of the struggles of the workers. On being actually involved in a major confrontation, he saw how many contradictions were involved in the lives of the workers – and the Asian workers in particular. Hussain began to understand all his own shortcomings. Now he felt he was involved in a real struggle, whereas in the past it was a romantic attachment to a real and painful struggle.

'Brothers, we form a delegation from our own ranks this time. No treacherous swine will talk to management on our behalf.' As Ghulam said this, he was greeted with a roar of approval.

'We tell management that, if they think they can get away with sacking a third of us, they have another strike coming. We will not accept the loss of a single job. We'll all go on strike!

'No. We'll have to go further than that. We'll have to sit in here – occupy the mill. And when the management come, we'll *gherao* them. If our workers back home can *gherao* their bosses – in a hail of bullets – then we can take on whatever they throw at us. It won't be easy, but we'll win.

'The overlookers can hear and I'm sure they are traitors. And I'm sure that there are others here who will go running to management and tell them what I'm saying and whatever we decide.'

No sooner had Ghulam said this than all eyes turned to the night jobber who felt his blood pressure rise and his body fill with fear.

'We'll give management one week to change their minds. Although they haven't officially told us, we all know and we won't play their games. We need time to organize ourselves also. Brothers, this time we have nothing to lose.' When Ghulam finished, he was greeted by the applause of jubilant resistance.

Hussain then explained briefly in English what Ghulam had just said. He was no longer worried about coming forward. It was now very clear that he would be amongst the first to be fired. He felt immense admiration for Ghulam and for his relationship with the workers and the simplicity with which he spoke. Gone was his romantic notion of struggle. Now he understood the struggle clearly and he was involved in it.

'You chaps better watch it,' a white supervisor said, half fearful of the numbers, half arrogant from his position. 'Mr Leach won't like this tone.' No one bothered to react to his threat. They all knew this would be the case.

'So, brothers, who's in favour of going ahead with what I've proposed?' Hussain repeated Ghulam's question in English.

For some time after this, a debate followed as to how they would organize and where, if they went on strike, they would get money to live on. Ghulam explained that they would have to force the Dyers and Bleachers Union to make this action official and pay them strike pay. He also said that the Union was racist through to the core, and that it was very corrupt and that they should not pin too many hopes on them. They would have to elect a committee to coordinate their action and the committee would have to look at ways of raising money.

When the time came for the vote, all but the jobber's hand went up from the black workers. The white workers blushed with embarrassment. When none of them raised their hands to go along with the strike and possible occupation of the mill, the black workers began to whistle and jeer them. From this turn, it was clear that violence could break out at any moment. The atmosphere in the room changed to anger. The black workers knew that the reason none of the whites voted was that they knew their jobs were safe.

'You're all mad!' a white supervisor shouted. 'No way is the Union going to support an extremist like Azad. You'll see sense when Mr Leach gets to hear about this!' After his comment, all the white workers left the meeting amidst shouts and taunts.

'Scum!' shouted Hussain at the top of his voice, but this was drowned by shouts of *'Dallay! Dallay!'*

Once the strike committee had been elected, the meeting closed to uproarious applause and expressions of solidarity, rebellion and resistance.

For most of the rest of the day, the overlookers and supervisors were in the manager's office, discussing what had happened. All the black workers were aware that sitting amongst them was the night-shift jobber.

Hussain had been filled with delight as the meeting of the workers had progressed. When he saw the old winder agree with all of them without hesitation, knowing he would probably be amongst those dismissed, Hussain had found a deep respect for the old man. On his way home, he hardly noticed the scenery. Usually, as they drove home, Hussain would sink back in the seat and watch, with deep relaxation as they drove past fields with cattle grazing. Today, his head was full of the coming struggle.

The driver broke the silence. 'Mr Leach said that he won't be seeing Ghulam again.'

'Well, let's see them try and give him the sack! We'll all stand by him! If they so much as touch him, we'll have a sit-in at the mill. That's what he'd want, brother!' Hussain's words hung in the air, as though they alone were enough to ward off the threats of the management. 'Anyway, not to worry.' Hussain continued, 'we'll see him on Monday. In the meantime, let's get this weekend over. It's probably the last one before we have to go on strike anyway. We know that they will say no, so there is really no other way than what brother Ghulam has suggested.'

No one spoke for the rest of the journey. Their silence expressed their anxiety and fear. More important, their silence expressed their resolve to battle and take on whatever was sent. Now they had nothing to lose and everything to gain.

In the early hours they came for him. Ghulam B. Azad was still in bed, lost in deep sleep, building his strength for the coming struggle at work.

When he arrived in England in 1969, he had not gone through the machinery of immigration. Like many thousands of others, he had stopped worrying about his status as he was covered by the 1971 amnesty. For all intents and purposes, he had lived, since 1971, under the impression that he could not be arrested in the early morning by the immigration police and quietly deported.

They came for him. No flashing beacons. No loud sirens. They knocked at his door. Half asleep, he answered. He heard his wife shouting after him, asking who was knocking them up at this time of the morning. When he saw them, his body froze in fear.

They introduced themselves briefly and said they would like to ask him some questions. Without waiting, they barged in past him and entered the house. He shouted a protest that they could not enter without a warrant. 'We don't need any warrants,' a tall one said. He had the air of an arrogant and omnipotent god. 'Sit down and answer a few questions. The rest we'll get out of you at the station,' the tall one thundered down at Ghulam.

His wife had come down, shouting and swearing at them. 'Calm down, madam,' the god-like devil ordered, 'this does not concern you.'

After a house search and a painful interrogation, they took Ghulam outside to a waiting police car and drove away, long before the neighbourhood had risen for the new day. Following the car in which Ghulam was taken, his wife's cries of confusion, pain and anguish.

The sleep of many a working-class black has been shattered by the knock of immigration police. Ghulam B. Azad was merely one more person who had been lured away from the country of his birth and his loved ones by promises of a better life, only to end up inside the high walls of British gaols. All over the country the hounds of the immigration authorities would wreak havoc and fear among those who lived with the dagger of deportation pointed at their hearts. Even those fortunate enough to have gone through the correct machinery lived in fear for themselves. After all, a new regulation could be introduced at any time, without anyone getting to hear about it.

Long before the neighbourhood woke up, Ghulam B. Azad was in a police station, answering the questions of his interrogator.

'I have a right to remain silent.'

'Look, boy, you watch too much television! You have no such fucking right. When we ask the questions, you answer!'

The news of Ghulam's arrest spread through the community. Some reacted in anger, others felt frightened; some day it could be them caught in the clutches of this machinery, whisked away from loved ones on a cold and lonely morning.

'What to do if you are taken away by the immigration authorities?' This was a question people often asked. There was no recourse available for defence in court to prove innocence. Whenever someone from the Home Office gave an interview, people viewed it as a joke. Another joke was media comment on the right of appeal against the decisions of immigration officials. What they never openly explained was that you could appeal only after you had been deported.

Workers at the mill were shocked by the news of Ghulam's arrest. They began to feel that they had better watch their step. No longer were they facing just the prospect of losing their jobs. A new dimension had been thrown into the struggle. They would ask themselves, 'Was it coincidence that Mr Leach said we would not see Ghulam again?'

When Hussain heard of the arrest, he had gone to the police station accompanied by Jalib and Mohan. Luckily, they arrived in time – Ghulam had not yet been taken to prison. The visit was very emotional.

Ghulam sat behind the thick plate-glass window which separated prisoners from visitors. His face was hardened to ensure that his friends did not see any signs of sorrow. The glass ensured that the prisoner found no consolation in physical contact with his loved ones.

On seeing Ghulam caged like a bandit, the three visitors were filled with sadness and frustration.

'Why can't we just break down these walls and free him now?' Jalib wondered as he saw before him a man who had always gone out of his way to be caring and polite to his people.

'Did they beat you, brother?' Jalib asked, feeling that if Ghulam had replied 'yes', he would not be able to restrain himself from lashing out at the next police officer he saw, or anyone who represented this oppressive authority.

'They don't need to,' Ghulam's voice came through the glass. The visitors listened intently, trying to see if they could detect sadness in it. 'This whole system is torture. They don't have to beat you, to break you. Come, lads, tears are no good.' Ghulam saw before him three young people he didn't really know at all shedding tears at his predicament.

'If there is anything we can do, please ask, Ghulam,' Hussain said, helplessly.

'You know why they are doing this to me, Hussain. It's because of the mill. They don't want our workers fighting back. That's why they bring these devils into our lives. They are trying to stop our struggle against the injustices at work. They want us to be all wrapped up in the immigration laws.' As Ghulam spoke, his visitors filled with confidence, for they could see that even from behind these walls of oppression the fire of resistance still raged in him.

'There is much that can be done,' Ghulam continued, after a brief pause. 'Make as much noise in the community as possible and get the people to fight, brother.' Ghulam began to talk quickly as he saw his precious fifteen minutes fly past second by second. As calmly as the situation would allow, he explained patiently that they should organize some kind of committee and protest against his arrest, making sure that it was put so that it was clear that this was not just an attack on him.

'There is no situation that can't be fought, brothers. It looks difficult. The more difficult a situation is, the harder we must fight it.' He asked Hussain not to let his work-mates down, and said they should continue with their plans for the struggle at work.

Chapter 18

The inaugural meeting of the youth association was scheduled for Sunday, the day after Ghulam B. Azad's arrest. About two hundred youths attended. No letters or leaflets had been distributed. Word of mouth had been used to mobilize them.

Jeeta still had the list of addresses of the IPYA and he had taken it upon himself to contact all the old members and supporters of the association, carefully avoiding all those he felt would insist on giving the organization an Indian bias.

After the aims and objects had been discussed by the meeting, an executive committee was elected. It was decided that the executive should sit down and draw up a plan of action for the new organization. Although the atmosphere had been animated, no one was very clear about how the organization should be structured.

'Comrades, yesterday one of my work-mates was arrested by the immigration police.' Hussain had gone to the front of the meeting and started to speak. He had, throughout the meeting, sat in the front row, occasionally getting up to put forward a view. He now spoke with immense passion and anger. 'You probably know him, Ghulam B. Azad. Some brothers who are here today, and myself, we went to see him yesterday in the Pig Shop.' Hussain continued to describe what, in his opinion, were the reasons for Ghulam's arrest. Although his voice was filled with emotion, his words came across clearly. He explained that it was a bit strange that Ghulam had been here all these years and yet, just when he was in the process of leading a very important struggle at work, he was arrested and placed under the threat of deportation. As Hussain talked, the meeting fell silent, that silence singing the anger of everyone there. They all felt that it wasn't just Ghulam B. Azad who was being put through this ordeal, but themselves as well. The silence spelt the signal of resistance. Each was thinking that something must be done.

'Can we just take this?' Hussain's voice roared across the meeting. It was greeted with a loud 'NO!'

'Burn Babylon, brother!' another voice shouted.

'All over the place, brothers, they are arresting hundreds of our people and quietly kicking them out of this country. When we went to see brother Ghulam yesterday, even from behind the cages of the Pig Shop, he said that we must fight. If they succeed in kicking him out of this country, he will be shot in Pakistan. When he was in Pakistan, he stood up against the regimes there. The cops know this.' Hussain explained that Ghulam had a long history of involvement with the resistance movement against various regimes in Pakistan and that deportation to Pakistan would certainly endanger his life.

'I say we should go out into the streets and fight against this injustice.' Hussain finished his speech. For a moment there was silence. Then, all of a sudden, the room exploded in loud applause.

The meeting began to discuss how Ghulam could be defended and how his deportation could be stopped. Although they were hardly organized, they were thrown immediately into a very difficult struggle. All present clearly understood that other avenues of fighting the deportation of Ghulam B. Azad were closed. Now that there was no other way to save him, they began to openly discuss ways of struggling beyond the confines of the non-existent laws.

Jalib's eyes were fixed closely on Jeeta, who had been chairing the meeting. Although his mind held images of grief and weeping for bygone moments, right now he was moving towards newfound strengths. Today he felt a satisfaction he had never before experienced. A satisfaction from the knowledge that all the times in the past when he had been overwhelmed with helplessness were now behind him. All around him were his friends and associates who shared the same frustrations. He listened intently to all that was being said. Sometimes, during the course of the meeting, he would float on the waves of the power he felt all of them could generate if only they could work together.

When his old friend Ranjit entered the room – it was years since he had seen him – he was filled with happiness. Ranjit's scars from the school battles were still clearly visible on his face. Jalib smiled and said to Ranjit it was good that the whites had not only knocked out his front teeth but had also paid for new ones. Jalib felt that times had not changed since the days when he and his friends experienced the running battles at school. The same menace which had united them in their many confrontations at school had once again drawn them together. But this time they were both conscious that the battle was no longer personal.

'Remember, brothers and sisters,' Jeeta said, 'when they needed us in this country? Was it Enoch Powell in fact who said, "Come to Britain where the streets are paved with gold"? I was walking down Lumb Lane the other day. I put my foot not on gold – we all know how much gold there is here – but in dog shit!' Laughter and applause. Jeeta felt it was not enough to just say that one of their people was in danger of being deported. It needed to be explained that it was not an accident of history that they were there. 'Nor is it a coincidence that they are trying to repatriate us now that the system is caught in the grips of crisis,' Jeeta continued.

'Compared to our countries, this land is indeed full of gold – these buildings and these factories. Mills and foundries – this is the gold they were talking about. This is our gold. God, didn't we give it to them! They stole it from many nations and peoples. It is our right to come here and live in peace. It's not a privilege that the white man is bestowing on us!

'Ghulam B. Azad has been living and working in this country for many years. His father and mother, like mine and yours, slaved for this country. He is here and here to stay!

'Remember also that when one of us is arrested on the suspicion of being what they call an illegal immigrant, you don't get charged, you just get kept in prison for as long as they like. You won't come before no court. Ghulam can't even appeal! No! That's wrong – the British are fair, so they tell the world – you can appeal, but only once you've been kicked out of here! They aren't going to allow brother Ghulam to appeal against their decision until he reaches Pakistan. Of course, after waiting a few years, he will lose, if he stays alive that long. But we are not going to let it come to that!'

Shaheen had been adamant that she would come to the meeting and she had, accompanied by Kiran. Shaheen would have felt very uncomfortable on her own, and she had had to argue a lot with Kiran to get her to come. But nothing on earth could have stopped her from being a part of this event which Jalib had talked of for so long.

On the night of the twenty-third, Shaheen had sat transfixed in front of the television screen, waiting for the ten o'clock news. The whole town had been talking about what had happened in Bradford during the day. She had trembled as she saw a friend flash on to the screen. She filled with anger as she saw another friend hit on the head by a mounted policeman; it made her heart miss a beat. She had so much wanted to be there, with her friends, fighting to defend her community. She had asked her parents whether she could go on the demonstration but they had laughed at her, saying, 'Surely you can't be serious? Anyway, you are about to become a *wohti*. This is no time to go on demonstrations!'

Shaheen had impatiently sat and waited for a glimpse of Jalib on the screen in front of her eyes. It would have made her so happy to see him. She had been filled with terror when she thought he might have been amongst those arrested. That night, she sat by her bedroom window for hours, waiting until she saw him come safely home. After that, she fell into a deep sleep, exhausted, as though she too had been on the streets, fighting the police who were doing everything in their power, it seemed, to ensure that the fascists had a safe and successful day.

Listening to the speeches about Ghulam B. Azad, she thought about Maqsood and the sort of life he was coming from. She felt it was not wrong for him to want to come to Britain. She too had felt the same about this country. It lured her people. What was wrong, she felt, as she heard Jeeta describe the reasons for her people coming here, was what they had to go through to get here. Jeeta's words made her think that her marriage was an acceptable method whereby Maqsood would escape the poverty of his life. True, it was also a custom and a part of her culture that was accommodating itself to a new problem. But much in her life seemed clearer.

She sat through the meeting and with the passing of every moment her determination grew. She would fight against Ghulam B. Azad's deportation too. She had wanted to stand up and talk about her own life and the life of many other girls like herself, but she could not find the courage to do so. Her courage and strength manifested themselves in her determination to find a solution to her coming marriage. When she had walked into the meeting, Shaheen had caught sight of Jalib. For a moment she had felt the stirring of love. They were both in the same room. But then she realized their common being had changed. Through coming to the meeting, Shaheen understood that in future she would not only concern herself with what went on in her own life, but she would struggle on behalf of all her people.

'I say, comrades,' Jeeta continued, 'that we form the Ghulam B. Azad Defence Committee. Get all the organizations of our community working on it and let the Home Office know that we won't take this lying down. We'll get people to send telegrams to the Minister, get petitions signed, call public meetings, hold a demonstration outside Armley gaol – that's where they've got him locked up. If they still don't let him out, we'll hold a national demonstration in this town! These MPs who come crawling around here when they want our votes – let's make them work. Let's get Ghulam's MP to go and see the Minister and put a question in Parliament. If we get enough people on the streets, no way will they deport him! If Ghulam is chucked out today, it will be one of us tomorrow. Ghulam B. Azad is here to stay. Deportation no way!' Jeeta's words echoed across the room amidst an avalanche of applause.

As Jeeta concluded, Jalib's eyes travelled to where his schoolfriend was sitting. Looking at Ranjit, he felt a closeness. Although they were no longer close friends, because Ranjit was here today, he felt a bond of togetherness. It was as though their school friendship had changed into something much stronger, something they had never been able to understand when they were children.

'It's not enough to ask just our community organizations to support Ghulam B. Azad. I say we ask anyone to support Ghulam. All the progressive white groups and white people should also come and support us in this struggle.'

Finally, it was agreed that the executive committee should also take up the question of deportations in a wider context. All progressive elements would be invited to join under an umbrella organization called Campaign against Deportations and Racist Immigration Laws (CADRIL). Thus, on its first day, the organization of the youth consciously thrust itself head-first into a struggle with the immigration authorities.

The meeting was almost over. Jalib had a strong feeling of achievement. For once, he felt, he had attended a meeting which had not ended, after a lot of emotive and animated speeches, in everyone going to the pub and drowning their militancy in the arms of Bacchus, eventually going home drunk, singing, 'We shall overcome', or some other such inebriated song.

At the end of the meeting Mohan described what he had seen in Southall. Although everyone was interested, the meeting had gone on too long and he was greeted with indifference. Also, he had been very nervous and this had not helped his presentation. When he sat down, Jalib teased him, telling him that in future he should work out what he was going to say, as no one had understood what the hell he had been talking about.

During the meeting, Shaheen had hardly noticed Jalib sitting there. She had been totally engrossed in the discussions taking place. Before coming to the meeting, she had spent hours trying to decide whether she should phone the Home Office secretly and tell them that she did not want to marry Maqsood, thereby preventing his entry into the country. When they talked about Ghulam's arrest, she had agreed that this injustice had to be fought. She had begun to see that the fascist marches in black communities, the newspapers churning out racist stories, the immigration police going around early in the morning picking people up, the politicians talking about immigration, were not separate issues but all connected by a bond of growing racism which had been dormant and was now being brought to the fore. This realization put her through yet more agonizing as to what she should do in order to find a solution to her coming doom.

When the meeting finished, all its participants departed in small groups, each one talking excitedly about the possibilities of their newly found strength. Shaheen and Jalib exchanged glances to say goodbye.

Chapter 19

Maqsood finally arrived. On the day Shaheen had gone to Heathrow Airport, she had been full of fear and embarrassment. She loathed every moment of what she had gone through. Since Maqsood's arrival, she had met Jalib only once and then very briefly. They were overcome with anguish and neither of them could say very much. There wasn't, after all, much to say. They had both known that the day would come when Maqsood would arrive. Their meeting was a very emotional farewell. For once she had not cared if her lover saw her cry. They both wept in the company of their loneliness.

Maqsood had been staying with relatives and had not had much to do with Shaheen. She always managed to avoid him whenever he came to her home. The fact that he was here in person would be enough to put her through tantrums. Before, she could hardly sleep because of worry. Now, even her dreams were haunted by her approaching marriage. The marriage at the Registry Office had already taken place. Only the Islamic ceremony remained.

'At least I'm still me for a few more weeks,' she would tell herself, trying to bring some comfort and relaxation into her life. She no longer really thought about what was happening, but simply went along.

Each night her house would be filled with women, sitting in the front room around a *dholki*, singing songs about love, marriage and other subjects which would mock Shaheen's state of mind and her predicament. Sometimes, when she was trying to hide herself away from all the prying eyes, someone would call her down and they would start to sing songs about her. Although on each occasion she would try to return a smile of gratitude, in reality whenever her name was mentioned in the context of a song she would fill with pain. She would awkwardly excuse herself and go and sit in her dark room, unable to face putting on the lights, because she did not want to see the henna patterns on her hands.

149

A date had been fixed for the Islamic ceremony. It was due to be held in three weeks' time. The time Shaheen had left brought her no relief or comfort. She had stopped feeling sorrowful, becoming inured to the pain and anguish of the past. Although she still fought hard inside herself, in order not to hurt her parents, she was determined that she would go only so far. Although she had gone through the 'English' marriage at the Registrar's Office, she had considered it a stupid irrelevance.

The campaign for Ghulam's release was making good progress. Posters decorated every available board in and around the city. Numerous organizations had come together under the banner of CADRIL. The Youth Movement and some other local black organizations were represented in the Ghulam B. Azad Defence Committee, which provided leadership for the campaign. Already a demonstration had taken place outside Armley gaol, where he was being held. Wherever one looked, posters shouted 'Free Ghulam B. Azad – State Attacks on Black People Must Stop'.

Although so much support had been generated for him, there was still no indication from the Home Office that they were prepared to give Ghulam his freedom. The campaign now revolved around a national demonstration. Petitions had been handed to the Minister. There had been a well-attended public meeting. The town had been buzzing with activity.

The feast was over. The wedding songs hung ghost-like in the air. Shaheen sat silently in her room. The silence was broken at regular intervals as a tear fell on her crisp new bed-sheets. She felt her enslavement complete. There was only one night left now and then she would start her life with Maqsood.

Now the house was empty. Save for Shaheen and Maqsood. She sat apprehensively in her bedroom. Maqsood was downstairs. Everyone had left, making pathetic excuses about being busy for the day. Her heartbeat bounced off the walls of her bedroom and out into the fresh, free air of summer. She felt like jumping out of her window and ending her life. Contradictory emotions crashed around in her head and stomach: confusion, pain, sorrow. She heard a door creak downstairs. Her body went cold, knowing Maqsood was about to come up. A long distance

150

from the sound of Shaheen's weeping, the angry noise of the demonstration could be heard. The chants could be heard faintly through her window,

'FREE GHULAM B. AZAD. GHULAM B. AZAD IS HERE TO STAY – DEPORTATION NO WAY!'

Shaheen had changed out of her *dulhan*'s clothing. It had been soaked in her tears and those of her mother. She heard Maqsood's footsteps coming up the stairs and paced the room like a caged beast of prey. Now her mind was set. She felt there was only one thing left to do. She was no longer frightened. This was her life! She had accepted so far her parents' requests. She clasped her hands and wiped the sweat on her *kurta*.

Maqsood knocked on the door. She covered her head with the *dupatta* and walked to the window to look out, into the distance. She felt his presence in the room. After some hesitation, she turned and looked him straight in the eyes. For a moment, all her thoughts left her and with them, her confidence and determination. Maqsood stood in front of her, perplexed as to why she was behaving like this. He assumed that she must be bashful. The room went silent. Only their heartbeats, each singing a different tune, broke the silence.

'I'm sorry. I don't know how to put this, Maqsood,' her voice broke. She struggled to grab some breath. She was determined that no more tears would roll down her face. 'I never wanted to marry you. It's not my fault. It's nothing personal. I don't want to hurt you . . .'

Maqsood opened his mouth to say something but was unable to. Even at a distance, he felt the anger and determination radiate from her body. His mind was filled with confusion. He thought that perhaps this was what Western education did to Asian girls. He began to sense the next sentence, and filled with fear that maybe they would deport him, with all his dreams of a better life.

'No, please. Don't say anything. Just listen. I hope you will understand. Please try to understand. You're here now. If I say no, they'll kick you out. I don't want to do that. I didn't want to hurt my mother and father so I went along. I don't want to live with you as your wife. I'm sorry.' She did not realize, but she was shaking as she said these words. Maqsood stood, speechless.

'You're here and you should stay here, in England, I mean. You didn't marry me but a chance of a better life . . .' They looked at each other in silence. Maqsood understood what Shaheen was saying. He could find no words to argue with her. The tone of her voice told him that she had gone through many tormenting moments in order to say this. The silence of their company was broken by the loud noise of the demonstration as it came nearer Shaheen's house.

'Out there my friends are shouting for their rights. I don't know what you think of this country but it's bad. I want to be myself not just a wife. I'm going to join them.' She walked past Maqsood. 'Please try to understand.' Without waiting for a reply, she hurriedly left the room and ran towards the demonstration as it passed the street corner.

A few days after the demonstration, it was announced by the Home Office that they had changed their minds and would give Ghulam B. Azad indefinite leave to remain in Britain. On hearing the news, Jalib and Mohan ran hysterically around the streets, shouting and singing in jubilation.

On the day of the victory party, Jalib sat on his own, when all around him his friends were celebrating and being merry. He had just learned that his cousin had been arrested in Birmingham and deported.

'Before brother Azad speaks to us, I'd like to call brother Hussain to the platform,' Jeeta announced through the microphone, over the heads of the people. 'He will read the poem that he and brother Jalib wrote after seeing Azad in prison.' Jalib raised his head as Hussain walked to the platform.

As Hussain approached the rostrum, he walked with an air of ecstatic jubilation. It had taken the youth, backed by their community, many months to free Ghulam.

The workers at the mill had been saddened and horrified at Ghulam's arrest and imprisonment. No sooner had Ghulam gone than all light in their lives went with him. One third of the workers at the Mill had been made redundant, among them Hussain. Without the support of Ghulam, Hussain had been unable to organize the workers to resist the management's tactics of intimidation. The rumour had spread that the workers should learn from what had happened to Ghulam. The workers were filled with so much fear that they had not met together again to protest against the redundancies. Hussain and the others had been thrown on the dole.

Without adding any comments to Jeeta's introduction, Hussain began to read from a piece of paper.

'We've called it, "The Carrot and the Whip". It is clear why this is the name. We hope you like it.'

'They dangled the Carrot of the Gold you'd find
You bit it –
You'll work in the factories and mills all the time.
Like a great beast of burden you'll clock on the hours
in the days and in the nights.
In the Mummy of democracies
and the Daddy of hypocrisies –
Where are your rights?

'Flashy scenes
On telly screens
Of the things you should buy
With the money you don't have.

'You're down and depressed
Tired and repressed
Your taxes you've paid
A knock on your door
Just another fishing raid!
They'll make the people think
You're just another crook
You'll never get to know
The worm on the hook.

'When you try to resist
They're just a bit quick
They'll dangle the Carrot
(Don't bite!)
And give you the Whip.

'Thank you for listening.' Hussain walked off the stage amidst some laughter and a lot of applause.

'Brothers and sisters. I thank everyone who has struggled in my name. There is not the word in my command.' Azad spoke in

Punjabi, over the heads of many people who had become totally silent to hear of the experience of the man they had all fought to free.

'They've gone so far with this racist machinery that now even white people are not safe. When I was locked up in the gaol, the worst thing was that there are so many of our people in there. Locked up like thieves and bandits. They haven't stolen or robbed – but have been robbed in the mills for so long. Then, they didn't care how they got someone to come and work at their ageing machines. They desperately needed our labour. Now, they say that anyone with black skin must be either a thief or else an illegal immigrant!

'White people must remember that racism is used against us today but tomorrow it will be white people who are caught in the grip of this monster. Then it will be too late. They must fight now.

'I met a man from New Zealand. A white man. He had been in Armley gaol for over six months on suspicion of being an illegal immigrant. I told him to apply for bail. He told me he had. You'll never believe what happened to this poor lad. The prosecution stood in front of the magistrate and said, "We object strongly to this man being given bail on the grounds that he will leave the country!" ' The audience roared with laughter. 'The magistrate then said, "Right, then, send him down." The poor man is still there and doesn't even know how to get deported!

'Finally, brothers and sisters, we must not stop here. It has been a big lesson for us all. Whenever any of us is facing deportation, or our families are not allowed to live together, then we must take our case to our people. We can force victory on them, even when we do not think there is any chance. I didn't think at first that I would see daylight again. But when the campaign started, then I was sure that if the people supported me, then I would win. I thank everyone who has helped me.'

Soon everyone dissolved into the flow of music. The tension and energy that had gone into the campaign now danced on the floor. No sooner had the families left the celebration than the bar opened and those still there crowded around it. With alcohol bouncing in their blood, everyone danced in jubilation.

Although he had not been invited to attend the victory celebration, as he had not in any way supported the campaign for the

154

freedom of Azad, the chief community relations officer had come. He was standing at the bar, buying drinks for the leadership of the Youth Movement, and all those who stood near them. With him came his friend, from the Commission for Racial Equality.

'Of course, Jeeta,' the community relations officer continued, 'the Commission gives grants to self-help groups. In fact, we keep a keen eye open for any new groups that come up. We'll be only too happy to assist if your organization wants to use our services.' His friend from the Commission nodded slyly in agreement. 'In fact, Prince Charles is coming to Bradford soon,' the friend from the Commission said, 'perhaps you would like to meet him?'

The mention of Prince Charles made Jalib angry. He had just come to sit with them, sensing that one of them would be going to the bar soon as their glasses were almost empty, and he had no more money. Mohan too had joined them and stood in anger at the mention of Prince Charles's name.

'What the hell we want to meet him for? He is supposed to be the prince of a country that is doing this to us, and you say we should meet him! Shit this! I ain't going to meet him. No way, man!' Mohan and Jalib walked away in a huff.

'Some of our lads get a bit angry,' said Jeeta. 'I think it's a good idea. But it's not my choice. The organization will have to discuss it. I suppose it's a good way to get respectability.'

Although Jeeta saw no reason for not meeting Prince Charles, he was aware that some people would object very strongly.

The two representatives continued to explain in great detail what they were all about and how they could help. They explained that they had given sizeable grants to the Southall Youth Movement, among others.

'Some people think we are trying to buy groups off with the money we give. But I think that the money is there and the ethnic minorities should use it.' The way the representative spoke gave the impression that he knew the truth of the matter but had learned to speak like a friend to hurt and angered strangers. He had been through many meetings such as this.

Jeeta, Hussain and Harjosh were by now thoroughly intoxicated, both by the alcohol and the victory that the Youth Movement had just achieved. They were too full of the rebellion of youth to think the sober thoughts of experience.

When the discussion to decide on a meeting with Prince Charles did take place, much later, Jeeta did not participate. By not speaking against the visit, he clearly manoeuvred matters so that he would go and meet the Prince.

Only years later did these young Asians understand that, even if the state was pouring huge amounts of money into the emerging movement, it was a small price to pay to buy off the militancy of a people's struggle.

Find out more about Penguin Books

We publish the largest range of titles of any English language paperback publisher. As well as novels, crime and science fiction, humour, biography and large-format illustrated books, Penguin series include *Pelican Books* (on the arts, sciences and current affairs), *Penguin Reference Books, Penguin Classics, Penguin Modern Classics, Penguin English Library* and *Penguin Handbooks* (on subjects from cookery and gardening to sport), as well as *Puffin Books* for children. Other series cover a wide variety of interests from poetry to crosswords, and there are also several newly formed series – *King Penguin, Penguin American Library* and *Penguin Travel Library*.

We are an international publishing house, but for copyright reasons not every Penguin title is available in every country. To find out more about the Penguins available in your country please write to our U.K. office – Dept EP, Penguin Books Ltd, Harmondsworth, Middlesex UB7 0DA – unless you live in one of the following areas:

In the U.S.A.: Dept DG, Penguin Books, 299 Murray Hill Parkway, East Rutherford, New Jersey 07073.

In Canada: Penguin Books Canada Ltd, 2801 John Street, Markham, Ontario L3R 1B4.

In Australia: Marketing Department, Penguin Books Australia Ltd, P.O. Box 257, Ringwood, Victoria 3134.

In New Zealand: Marketing Department, Penguin Books (N.Z.) Ltd, P.O. Box 4019, Auckland 10.

In India: Penguin Overseas Ltd, 706 Eros Apartments, 56 Nehru Place, New Delhi 110019.

Also published by Penguins

JULY'S PEOPLE
Nadine Gordimer

It is war. For years the situation has been 'deteriorating'. Now all over South Africa the cities are battlegrounds. Bam and Maureen Smales – enlightened, liberal whites – are rescued from the terror by their servant, July, who leads them to refuge in his native village.

What happens to the Smales, and to July, mirrors the changes in the world – and gives us glimpses into a chasm of hatred and misunderstanding.

'A brave and imaginative book and should be read' – *Listener*

'Adventurous, powerful and despairing' – *Financial Times*

'It is so flawlessly written that every one of its events seems chillingly, ominously possible' – *The New York Times Book Review*

BEDBUGS
Clive Sinclair

'If you're interested in compellingly unpleasant but brilliantly written short stories, then you will sit up all night with Clive Sinclair's latest collection. Your sleep (when it comes) will then be interspersed with nightmares about stabbings, rape, treachery, illness, blood, revenge and death . . .' – *Yorkshire Post*

'Disconcerting brilliance, crazy humour and perfect control . . . He threads together West Coast argot, psychiatrists' newspeak, Yiddish, Hebrew, and can casually pop in an overheard exchange in a Cambridge -pub so that it sounds just as outlandish' – *Observer*

'Words come flying up at you from all angles . . . marvellously funny . . . he will make you laugh aloud' – *Punch*

Also published by Penguins

TSOTSI
Athol Fugard

Tsotsi is a white man's vision of the black ghetto, seen with nightmare clarity – 'an engrossing psychological thriller which is certainly one of the best novels in South African fiction' – *The Times Literary Supplement*

In the shadows of Sophiatown in South Africa stalks Tsotsi, the gangster, bringing pain and terror. Derelict, deprived, nihilistic, he treats life as it has treated him until a chance encounter with a woman leaves him holding a life in his hands: and into the parched and agonized territory of Tsotsi's soul is born a strange redemption.

Written twenty years ago by Fugard, the world-famous dramatist, *Tsotsi* has only recently been published – a novel as timeless and terrible in its portrayal of injustice as *Cry, the Beloved Country*.

UNION DUES
John Sayles

In the late sixties in West Virginia a seventeen-year-old youth runs away from home ... His father goes after him, abandoning his fellow miners in their bitter struggle against union corruption ...

Through father and son we enter worlds where the young idealist challenges society and the older blue-collar worker fights exploitation. *Union Dues* is a brilliantly thought-provoking story of the American Dream as it really is: a harsh battle for survival – involving love and betrayal, hope and despair, sacrifice and commitment – all the dues that life exacts.